UNSTOPPABLE
AFFIRMATIONS
FOR TEENS

UNSTOPPABLE AFFIRMATIONS FOR TEENS

31 DAYS OF WORDS THAT TRANSFORM YOUR MIND AND LEVEL UP YOUR LIFE

LOU JONES

Unstoppable Affirmations for Teens: 31 Days of Words that Transform Your Mind and Level Up Your Life
Copyright © 2024 by Lou Jones

Published in Dallas, Texas, by Let's Go! Press

All rights reserved. No part of this publication may be reproduced, stored in a retrieval system, or transmitted in any form or by any means—electronic, mechanical, photocopy, recording, or any other—except for brief quotations in critical reviews or articles, without the prior permission of the publisher.

Unless otherwise stated, all Scripture quotations are taken from the Holy Bible, New International Version®, NIV®. Copyright © 1973, 1978, 1984, 2011 by Biblica, Inc.® Used by permission. All rights reserved worldwide.

Scripture quotations marked (KJV) are taken from King James Version (KJV): King James Version, public domain.

Scripture quotations marked NLT are taken from the New Living Translation, copyright © 1996, 2004, 2015 by Tyndale House Foundation. Used by permission of Tyndale House Publishers, Inc., Carol Stream, Illinois 60188. All rights reserved.

ISBN 978-1-7364439-4-1 (paperback)

Library of Congress Control Number: 2024914741

Printed in The United States
10 9 8 7 6 5 4 3 2 1

This books is dedicated to every teenager.
May you laugh loud, dream even louder,
and conquer the world (with a good playlist
in the background, of course).

CONTENTS

Foreword...**xiii**
Introduction: Level Up Your Life.................................**xvii**

Affirmations to Level Up Your Purpose and Priorities

Day 1: Affirmations for Discovering Your Purpose...................**3**
Day 2: Affirmations for Academic Excellence.......................**9**
Day 3: Affirmations for Exam Success..................................**13**
Day 4: Affirmations for Athletic and
    Extracurricular Achievement...................................**17**

Affirmations to Level Up Your Spirit and Soul

Day 5: Affirmations to Grow Spiritually.............................**23**
Day 6: Affirmations to Embrace Your Identity.....................**27**
Day 7: Affirmations to Increase Self-Love, Self-Esteem,
    and Self-Worth..**31**
Day 8: Affirmations to Overcome Negative and
    Suicidal Thoughts..**39**
Day 9: Affirmations to Become More Grateful and Thankful...**45**

CONTENTS

Affirmations to Level Up Your Attitude and Confidence

Day 10: Affirmations to Believe in Yourself..........................**51**
Day 11: Affirmations to Increase Confidence........................**57**
Day 12: Affirmations to Resist Peer Pressure and Drug Use.....**61**
Day 13: Affirmations to Overcome Fear.............................**65**
Day 14: Affirmations to Overcome Bullying.........................**69**

Affirmations to Level Up Your Family and Friendships

Day 15: Affirmations for Positive Parent and
          Family Relationships...**75**
Day 16: Affirmations for Healthy Friendships......................**81**
Day 17: Affirmations for Dating and a Future Spouse............**85**
Day 18: Affirmations for Healing a Broken Home................**91**

Affirmations to Level Up Your Health and Wellness

Day 19: Affirmations for Health, Healing, and Wellness........**97**
Day 20: Affirmations for Physical Purity...........................**101**
Day 21: Affirmations for Better Mental Health...................**105**
Day 22: Affirmations for Overcoming Depression...............**109**
Day 23: Affirmations for Improving Your Body Image..........**113**

CONTENTS

Affirmations to Level Up Your Success and Future

Day 24: Affirmations for Developing a Success Mindset........**119**
Day 25: Affirmations for Achieving Your Goals...................**123**
Day 26: Affirmations for College Success..........................**125**
Day 27: Affirmations for Your Future Career......................**129**

Affirmations to Level Up Your Productivity

Day 28: Affirmations to Overcome Social Media
and Gaming Dependence..**135**
Day 29: Affirmations to Take Personal Responsibility.............**139**
Day 30: Affirmations to Overcome Procrastination...............**143**
Day 31: Affirmations to Get a Job and Shine.......................**147**

Bonus Chapters

Affirmations for Abundance and Prosperity.......................**153**
Affirmations for Entrepreneurial Success...........................**159**
Affirmations for Staying Focused...**165**
Affirmations for Letting Go of Stress, Worry, and Anxiety......**169**
Affirmations for Better Self-Care...**173**
Affirmations for Healing a Broken Heart............................**177**
Affirmations for Letting Go and Moving Forward................**181**

About the Author..**185**
Acknowledgements...**187**
References..**189**

FOREWORD

OH hey! THERE I'm so pumped you're checking out this book, *Unstoppable Affirmations: 31 Days of Words that Transform Your Mind and Level Up Your Life*. Not only am I the author's super-supportive spouse, but I've also seen firsthand the amazing impact these affirmations can have.

Let's rewind. This book started with my husband, the mastermind behind all these affirmations. We're a team, always pushing each other to be our best. Affirmations aren't just fancy words for us - they're like cheat codes for success! They are a part of our winning formula for individual achievements and shared success.

Personally, affirmations helped me crush my goals. From achieving financial goals to landing my dream job, they were one of my secret weapons. I remember saying an affirmation every day about making a ton of money (think six figures!), and guess what? I did it in just five years! Through all the ups and downs, affirmations helped me ditch negative thoughts and go after what I truly wanted.

Dating drama? Been there! Back then, I encouraged myself to stay focused and wait for God's best with an affirmation (similar to the "Affirmations for Dating and a Future Spouse" in this book). Fast forward, and here I am, happily married to the love of my life!

Witnessing the power of affirmations firsthand is why I'm so excited for you to read this book. The author isn't just some stuffy expert – he's a coach, and former youth pastor of 15+ years, who genuinely wants to help you reach your full potential. This book is his way of sharing his knowledge and passion for affirmations, and how they can seriously change your life.

Face it, the world can be pretty tough. Negativity, self-doubt, and all that drama can really bring you down, if you let it. That's why a positive mindset is key! This book isn't just pages and words – it's a toolkit filled with affirmations designed to tackle everything from school stress to building confidence.

Wanting to try out for the varsity team and feeling those pre-tryout jitters? We've got you covered! This book has affirmations specifically designed for athletic success and extracurricular activities. Feeling like you want to build stronger friendships but don't know where to start? This book has affirmations to help you create positive connections! With sections on academics, relationships, purpose, and more, there's truly something for everyone.

Here's the coolest part: Over the next 31 days, you're not going at it alone. These affirmations will dig deep and become a part of you.

So, awesome reader, get ready to unlock the power of affirmations! Commit to the daily routine, and watch your life transform. Trust me, the words you speak have a ton of power.

Here's to your journey of becoming UNSTOPPABLE!

Author of *Living the Sweet Life*
@ruthjonesinspires

INTRODUCTION

Level Up Your Life

I clearly recall, as a teenager, going on vacation and swimming in the ocean for the first time. Just before I plunged into the water, my mom warned me about rip currents—powerful currents that can pull even the strongest swimmers into turbulent waters. Kind of scary, right?

Well, guess what? Our world can be like that rip current, dragging us down with negativity. News blasts us with drama, social media is full of comparison traps, and even our own brains love to focus on the bad stuff. It's no wonder tons of teens struggle with stress, anxiety, and feeling like they're just not good enough.

But here's the awesome part: you don't have to get swept away! There's a secret weapon successful people use to crush their goals and live amazing lives, and it's totally accessible to you too. **It's called affirmations.** Think of them as super-charged statements you say to yourself that rewrite your brain for success.

Here's the deal: our brains are like computers, and are kinda wired for negativity. We naturally focus more on the bad stuff – that test you bombed, the fight with your BFF, or the endless stream of trolls online. But affirmations can change that! By saying positive things about yourself and your goals on a regular basis, you can actually reprogram your brain to believe them. It's like giving yourself a daily pep talk that boosts your confidence and helps you win against negativity. Sounds pretty awesome, right?

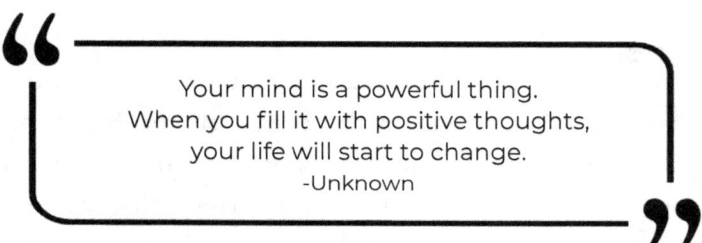

> Your mind is a powerful thing.
> When you fill it with positive thoughts,
> your life will start to change.
> -Unknown

The world's negativity doesn't have to drown out your light. **This book is packed with tons of affirmations for everything you deal with as a teen**: school, friendships, relationships, dreams, and future plans. There are even sections to help you deal with anxiety and that voice in your head telling you you're not good enough. Plus, you'll learn how to use affirmations effectively to get the most out of them.

If you're wanting more confidence, happiness, and success in life, this is the one technique that will supercharge your results. **My story is proof that affirmations work!**

How Affirmations Helped Change My Life's Story

I used to be that teen who felt lost and unsure of myself. I was 12, living in the heart of Detroit, and I had a big, BIG secret: I couldn't read. It didn't matter how many tutors I tried or fancy private schools I went to, books were like a whole other language to me. I had failing grades, and to cope with the pressure and shame, I became quiet and withdrawn and even dabbled in drugs. My life was headed down the wrong path and fast.

Then, in seventh grade, a game-changer happened. My mom found this amazing community reading program that finally cracked the code for me, and I learned how to read. But even with this new skill, I still felt like a total loser. I still had failing grades, low self-esteem, and a bad attitude—the whole package.

One day, I was reading the Bible (props to Mom for that too!), and I came across the story of David and Goliath, and I saw something I had never seen before. This dude, David, was facing this towering giant, and everyone thought he was toast. But guess what David did in the face of overwhelming odds? He didn't freak out, but spoke aloud a positive affirmation of victory over his life.

Basically, he said, "I took down a lion, I beat a bear, this giant doesn't stand a chance against the awesome God I have on my side!"

Whoa! David's confidence and the power of his words totally hit me. It was like a lightbulb moment.

Here's this guy, declaring his past wins and believing God for victory. That's when I realized the power of speaking positive things over my life.

So, I started doing the same thing. I would say stuff like, "If David can do it, I can do it too!" or "I can get better grades!" and "I'm a leader, not a follower!" The more I spoke positive words over my life, the more I actually started believing them. My confidence skyrocketed, and I knew I could achieve anything I set my mind to.

> The moment you accept responsibility for everything in your life is the moment you gain the power to change anything in your life.
> -Hal Elrod

With hard work, a ton of prayer, and those positive affirmations on repeat, I found the courage to turn my grades around and gained a new self-image. By the end of eighth grade, I was an award-winning honor roll student and recipient of the Spirit of Detroit Award for outstanding achievement and citizenship. Pretty sweet transformation, right?

A Teacher's Influence
Affirmations and Limitless Potential

High school was another game-changer for my affirmation journey. My history teacher, Mr. Lichtman, was like a positivity guru. His classroom was plastered with posters of awesome quotes and he even had us start each day by saying positive things about ourselves out loud. Sharing those affirmations with everyone, and seeing them all over the walls, made you really believe you could achieve anything. It was like a daily motivation boost that made me realize the power of speaking good stuff over myself.

By the time I graduated, I had a great GPA (3.5!), made it into the National Honor Society (so cool!), became president of the student government (whoa!), got accepted into a Big Ten college (dream come true!), and even scored a bunch of scholarships (cha-ching!). Leveling up my self-belief empowered me to strive for everything I was capable of.

If I hadn't discovered affirmations, things might have been way different. Remember how I was struggling before? With low self-esteem, shame, and dabbling in drugs? Yeah, that path probably wouldn't have led to all this awesomeness. My story is proof that positive self-talk is seriously powerful. It can change your whole mindset, boost your confidence, and help you ditch negativity for good. No matter what challenges you face, you don't have to let them hold you back. With affirmations, you can switch from feeling scared and inadequate to feeling determined and unstoppable. Pretty cool, right?

Unlock Your Awesome
A Guide to Becoming the Best You

Before I share with you all the amazing benefits of affirmations, let's cover some basics about what affirmations are and why they work.

⇾ What is an Affirmation, Anyway? ⇽

Think of an affirmation like a supercharged statement you say to yourself that flips your brain into positive mode. An affirmation is designed to stir up positive thinking and push you to achieve your greatest potential in life. Instead of battling negative thoughts that drag you down and tell you that you're not enough, affirmations fight back! By saying positive things about yourself on repeat, you can retrain your brain to believe them. Through repetition, your thoughts, feelings, attitudes, and actions begin to upgrade, transforming into new, positive beliefs.

This book is jam-packed with affirmations to tackle all sorts of things–from little things that might be bugging you, like exams and stress to really big things like dealing with a broken home or bullying. We're here for you! This is your toolbox filled with positivity power-ups to help you become unstoppable.

⇾ Why Affirmations Actually Work? ⇽

Did you know your brain has, like, 60,000 thoughts every day? Whoa, your brain is chatty. That's a lot! The bad news is, most of them (around 70%) tend to be negative. Ugh, right? These negative thoughts turn into negative words, which can bring you down and make you feel stressed or anxious. It's like a self-fulfilling prophecy – the more you think and say negative stuff, the more negative things seem to happen.

But here's the cool part: science says your words actually have power over your brain! Research on the brain found that one negative comment can set off a whole chain reaction in part of your brain (the amygdala), causing it to release stress neurochemicals that make you say even more negative things, making you feel worse—yikes! (Newberg & Waldman, 2006). But guess what? The opposite is true too.

By saying positive things about yourself (affirmations!), you can actually rewire your brain for the better. This boosts your confidence and helps you see the world in a more positive light. Think of your brain as dirty glasses. Negative self-talk is like grungy lenses that make everything seem dark. Affirmations are like clean glasses, brightening things up and showing you all the possibilities.

The Bible even talks about this! Proverbs 23:7 says, *"For as he thinketh in his heart, so is he"* (basically, your thoughts shape who you are). Ephesians 4:23 tells us to *"be renewed in the spirit of your mind"* (KJV). If you change your thoughts, you will change your words. Change your words, change your life. Pretty awesome, right? This book will teach you how to ditch the negativity and use affirmations to become the unstoppable you!

Rewire Your Mind
From "Ugh" to Unstoppable

Imagine trying to learn a new song on guitar. The first few times, it sounds rough, right? But the more you practice, the smoother you get. It's the same with affirmations.

A Look at the Research
The Science Behind Affirmations

- Feeling super stressed? Affirmations have been shown to reduce stress and its negative effect on your health (thanks, Sherman et al., 2009 & Critcher & Dunning, 2015!).

- Need a workout buddy? Affirmations have been used effectively in interventions to help people to be more physically active (big thanks to Cooke et al., 2014!).

- Feeling defensive; like nobody gets you? Positive affirmations can make you more open to accepting advice and help from others that you might normally find intimidating. (major props to Logel & Cohen, 2012).

- Want to be healthier? Affirmations can make you more open to health information and to improving healthy habits, such as eating fruits and veggies (high five to Harris et al., 2007 & Epton & Harris, 2008).

- Struggling in school? Research shows that consistent positive affirmations have been linked to better academic performance, especially for students who may be feeling left out (shoutout to Layous et al., 2017!).

- Feeling overwhelmed? Affirmations have been proven to lower stress and reduce overthinking (thanks to Koole et al., 1999 & Wiesenfeld et al., 2001).

- Feeling unsure of yourself? Affirmations can improve your self-worth and help you deal with life's uncertainties (big ups to Ruolei Gu et al., 2018).

The key to making affirmations work is saying them a LOT. Think of it like training your brain for positivity. Right now, your thoughts might be like bad habits you've had for ages. But with affirmations, you can replace those old habits with brand new, awesome ways of thinking. It's like upgrading the software in your brain.

> It's the repetition of affirmations that leads to belief. And once that belief becomes a deep conviction, things begin to happen.
> -Muhammad Ali

Here's an example: say you're scared of spiders (yuck!). If you keep telling yourself, "I'm terrified of spiders!" over and over, your brain starts to believe it even more. That's why seeing a spider makes you freak out – you've trained your brain to have a fear response. The same goes for negative self-talk like "I'm not good enough" or "I can't do it." The more you say it, the more you start to believe it, and that can totally mess with your confidence and motivation.

But here's the good news: you can break free from that negativity! By replacing those limiting thoughts with positive affirmations and saying them all the time, you can actually rewire your brain. It's like building new highways for positive thinking in your head. Sure, it might feel weird at first, but science says affirmations are totally legit! They can help you change your mindset and live a way more positive and powerful life. Pretty cool, right?

⇁ Positivity Power-Up ↽
10 Reasons Why Affirmations Rock

This book isn't just for teens who are struggling – it's for EVERYONE! Whether you're crushing life already or need a little help getting started, this is your guide to leveling up your awesomeness.

Here's how affirmations can be your secret weapon:

1. Positivity Party! – Affirmations help you ditch negativity and focus on the good stuff. They'll drown out those voices telling you you're not enough and help you embrace your amazingness!

2. Confidence Booster Shot! – Think of affirmations as your inner cheerleader. As you speak them, they build your confidence and make you feel like a total rockstar!

3. Smash Those Mental Roadblocks! – Ever feel stuck? Affirmations are your power tool to smash through limiting beliefs and show yourself you're capable of anything!

4. Silence the Inner Critic! – Picture affirmations as your shield against the negativity monster. They help you tell those negative thoughts to "take a hike!" and stay focused on your goals.

5. Keep Your Eyes on the Prize! – Affirmations remind you of the awesome things you're working towards. They're like a compass guiding you to a brighter future.

6. Control Your Thoughts! – Affirmations are like catchy tunes that get stuck in your head – but in a good way! They plant positive messages in your subconscious and make it a positive place. You end up more optimistic and ready to conquer anything.

7. Upgrade Your Emotional Well-Being! – Ready for some feel-good vibes all around? Affirmations promote self-love and acceptance, which helps you stress less and feel more amazing.

8. Live Your Best Life Ever! – Affirmations remind you of your strengths and make you feel empowered. The more you use them, the more positive you become, and that makes life way more fun!

9. Healthy and Happy Highway! – Affirmations can even improve your health, promote healing in your body and mind, and move you toward daily happiness. The more positive you are, the better you feel overall.

> Affirmations are our mental vitamins, providing the supplementary positive thoughts we need to balance the barrage of negative events and thoughts we experience daily.
> -Tia Walker

10. Bounce Back Like a Boss! – Affirmations help you build resilience. By telling yourself you can overcome anything, you'll see challenges as opportunities to grow and come back even stronger.

Using Affirmations
A Superpower, Not a Magic Wand!

Affirmations are awesome, but here's the deal: they're not a magic fix for everything. They can definitely help you deal with tough emotions and even stop negative thoughts, but they can't solve super serious problems on their own.

Think of affirmations like a cool sidekick, not a superhero. They're there to support you and boost your mood, but if you're facing something really big, like depression or a major challenge, it's important to get help from your parents and even a professional too. This could be a therapist, a psychiatrist, or even someone like a pastor if that feels right for you.

Remember, affirmations are a helpful tool, but they can't replace professional help when you really need it.

⇁ Affirmations and Faith ↽ Can You Use Both? (Totally!)

This is a question I get a lot, so let's break it down. Can you, as a Christian, use positive affirmations? Absolutely! But there are a few things to keep in mind:

1. The Bible is BIG on Words! The Bible talks a lot about the words we speak and how powerful our words are. Here are just a few mentions of the power behind the words we speak:

Wise words bring many benefits. -Proverbs 12:14 (NLT)

The words of the reckless pierce like swords, but the tongue of the wise brings healing. -Proverbs 12:18

The tongue has the power of life and death, and those who love it will eat its fruit. -Proverbs 18:21

For the mouth speaks what the heart is full of. A good man brings good things out of the good stored up in him, and an evil man brings evil things out of the evil stored up in him. But I tell you that everyone will have to give account on the day of judgment for every empty word they have spoken. For by your words you will be acquitted, and by your words you will be condemned." -Matthew 12:34b-37

So, affirmations can be a great tool to use your words for good!

2. Stay True to the Bible. Affirmations shouldn't go against what the Bible teaches. Affirmations that contradict what God asks us to follow in the Bible are wrong and do not belong in a Christians life. The Bible is our standard of truth, and in this book, you will find only affirmations that line up with God's word.

3. God is the Real Power Source not Us. Some new-age affirmations out there focus on your own strength or some "law of attraction" stuff. As a Christian, our trust is in God alone, His acceptance, and His desire for us to succeed, which is far greater than our own. Positive affirmations that are based solely on your strengths, personal discipline, and abilities alone are not enough. The source and power of our affirmations must be God's strength and not our own.

4. Neutral Affirmations Are Cool Too. There are some positive affirmations that don't directly mention the Bible but still fit with Christian values. (The fancy theologically term for this is "adiaphora.") Think things like "I embrace new opportunities" or "Today is going to be awesome!" These are great affirmations to use as a Christian teen.

Following these guidelines will help you use affirmations in a way that strengthens your faith and helps you grow as a person. Remember, affirmations are a tool, not a replacement for your relationship with God and genuine spiritual development. The coolest thing? I have another book in this series, specifically for teens, that focuses on the power of scripture declarations, which is like taking affirmations to the next level by speaking God's word!

How to Get the Most Out of This Book (Tips, Tricks and Hacks...Yes Please!)

Ready to unlock your awesomeness and level up your life? This book has you covered! Here's the deal: the affirmations inside can totally transform your life, but you gotta put them to work!

Don't wait — success starts NOW! Let's ditch the negativity and reprogram your brain for awesomeness. This book makes it super easy to focus on positive words and see the results for yourself. The affirmations are battle-tested and work on real teen problems (seriously!). Each chapter is packed with powerful words you can use in just a few minutes a day. That's why there are 31 chapters — one for every day of the month!

Here are some tips to get the most out of this book:

- **Keep it Handy!** Stash this book in your backpack, gym bag, or even on your nightstand, so you can easily pull it out when you need a

moment of mindfulness and positivity. There's also an ebook version for on-the-go positivity.
- **Choose Your Own Positivity Path!** Just because the chapters are numbered doesn't mean you have to read them in order. This book is your positive mindset boost, so flip to whatever chapter speaks to you right now! Feeling stressed about a test? Jump to the "Academic Excellence" and "Exam Success" affirmations. Need a confidence boost for a job interview? Head over to "Affirmations to Get A Job and Shine." You get the idea! Plus, there's a whole bonus section at the back of the book with even more hot topic affirmations! This book is all about what works for YOU. So go forth and conquer with the power of affirmations!
- **Sticky Note Power!** Write your favorite affirmations on sticky notes and stick them where you'll see them all day long.
- **Memory Master!** Memorize your favorites so you can easily recite them to yourself in clutch moments or whenever you need a confidence boost.
- **Rinse and Repeat is Key!** The more you say these affirmations, the more you reprogram your brain for success, happiness, and all-around good vibes.
- **Make it a Habit!** Do your affirmations first thing in the morning to start your day with the right mindset, before bed to end your day

with positive intention, on the ride to school, or anytime you need a pick-me-up. It's like self-care at your fingertips!

Ready to unlock your full potential and write your own epic success story? Then flip the page and dive into the world of affirmations! You were built for greatness, and affirmations are one of the keys to unlocking it. Let's become unstoppable, one positive word at a time!

Affirmations to Level Up Your Purpose and Priorities

DAY 1

Affirmations for Discovering Your Purpose

*If you can't figure out your purpose, figure out your passion.
For your passion will lead you right into your purpose.*
-Thomas Jakes

*You were put on this earth to achieve your greatest self,
to live out your purpose, and to do it courageously.*
-Steve Maraboli

I am open and ready to embrace my unique purpose.

I am actively uncovering my purpose.

I am in this world to discover and fulfill my purpose.

I am on the right path, and my purpose reveals itself to me at the perfect time.

I am an instrument of positive change, fulfilling my purpose in this world.

I am committed to becoming my best self.

I am open to experiences and people that support my purpose.

I am releasing myself from the pressure and stress of not knowing my purpose at this time in my life.

I understand that whether I call it my purpose, my calling, or my gift, it is essentially the same thing and will be revealed to me at the right time.

My mind is firmly fixed on achieving my purpose.

My written goals help me to live my purpose.

My future has a purpose and will exceed all of my hopes and expectations.

My purpose is clear to me now.

My life has meaning and is full of value.

My ability to conquer my challenges is limitless; my potential to succeed is infinite.

As I follow my passion, I will discover my purpose.

As I take action doing my passion, my life's purpose becomes clearer and clearer.

I live a creative life full of passion and purpose.

I have a strong sense of purpose that fuels my actions and decisions.

I have a burning desire to make a real difference in the world.

I have a clear vision of my purpose, and I actively pursue it.

I trust the process of discovering and living out my purpose.

I act with my purpose in mind and wonderful things happen as a result.

Once I discover my purpose, I will develop it.

Every day I am finding clues and hints that point to my purpose.

Living with purpose is one of the top priorities in my life.

Today I choose to move my life in the direction of my dreams.

When I follow my dreams, joy and prosperity accompany me in all that I do.

I am capable of achieving anything I set my mind to.

I am connected to my passion, which guides me towards my purpose.

I am worthy of living a life of purpose and fulfillment.

I am taking daily action to fulfill my ultimate purpose.

I am needed. I am important. What I do with my life matters.

I was born with the ability to develop my talents and skills for a reason.

I was born with a purpose, and it's waiting for me with open arms.

I seize every moment, and I put my words into action.

I am eager. I am energized. I am open. I am ready.

I am brave and committed to fulfilling my purpose.

I am excited to explore and embrace the abundant possibilities of my purpose.

I am grateful for the opportunities that align with my purpose.

I am finding ways to produce money that are in alignment with my passions and purpose.

I am capable of anything I set my mind to and anything I focus my energy towards.

I can fulfill my purpose. I will fulfill my purpose. I must fulfill my purpose.

I have the power to create a meaningful, passionate life for myself.

I have a purpose, and every day I discover more ways to live it.

My purpose aligns with my passions, talents, and values and contributes positively to the world.

My purpose brings joy, abundance, and positive impact to the world.

My purpose serves as a driving force that propels me towards greatness.

My purpose is a beacon that illuminates my path with clarity and certainty.

My purpose always keeps me motivated.

I release any doubts or fears that may hinder me from embracing my purpose fully.

Discovering my purpose will be one of the most exciting experiences of my life.

Every moment of every day I am becoming more and more certain of my purpose.

I awake each morning confident in knowing why I am on this planet.

I follow my own purpose, and let others follow theirs.

I honor my purpose by using my talents and abilities every day.

I honor my purpose by achieving my goals.

I invest time every day to work towards my purpose.

I know that I was born to fulfill an important and unique purpose.

I have great potential that I tap into every day.

The more fully I know myself, the clearer my purpose becomes.

I search within to discover what blocks my progress.

I take the time to understand and pursue my purpose.

I take time to find out what my real interests are.

I acknowledge that I have a purpose, and I am created for a unique reason.

My purpose is within me, but I must develop and nurture it.

Once I understand my purpose, I will use it to make the world a better place.

I am walking confidently towards my purpose. Every day I am taking steps to fulfill my potential.

I am fearless in the pursuit of my purpose because it's already mine.

I am open to receiving guidance to help me operate in my purpose.

I am patient and willing to wait in faith to understand the purpose for my life.

I was born with a God-given purpose, and I am ready to access it now.

I trust God to guide me towards my purpose and opportunities that align with it.

I refuse to settle for a life that is less than God's best for me.

DAY 2

Affirmations for Academic Excellence

*Find a subject that sets your soul on fire,
then learn everything about it.*
-Unknown

The more you learn, the more you earn.
-Warren Buffett

I am smart, talented, and creative.

I am capable of achieving academic excellence.

I am in control of my progress.

I am patient with myself as I learn new things.

I am a dedicated student, committed to my goals.

I am developing skills that will serve me for a lifetime.

I am resilient in the face of academic challenges.

The more I learn, the more I grow.

The more I learn, the more I achieve.

Learning is my superpower. Anything is possible.

Nothing can stop me from living the life of my hopes and dreams.

Today, I approach challenges with a positive and determined mindset.

I believe in my ability to understand and master any subject.

My mind's ability to learn and remember is increasing every day.

My mind absorbs and processes new information with great speed.

I am a leader in my own way, inspiring others to strive for excellence.

I am grateful for the support of my family, teachers, and friends.

I constantly expand my knowledge and understanding.

I pursue continuous learning and development.

I push myself to achieve higher grades, but I let go of the pressure to excel academically at the cost of my well-being.

Every day I am becoming a better student and a more confident individual.

My curiosity and creativity make learning exciting for me.

There is no reason for me to compare myself to others.

Today, I set aside my fears and take charge of my education and grades.

It's okay not to know everything. I can always learn.

I have a winner's mindset, and I will strive to do my best.

I embrace the discipline needed for academic success.

I turn my academic dreams into achievements.

I turn my goals into realities with discipline and effort.

I turn anxiety into determination and focus.

I celebrate every achievement, big or small.

I am a positive thinker, and I see solutions rather than problems.

I am a good listener, and I value the opinions of my teachers and peers.

I am on a journey of becoming a successful student.

I can easily balance learning and my social life.

I learn from my challenges and always find ways to overcome them.

I am surrounded by people who support and encourage me.

I am proud of myself for all that I have accomplished.

I love learning, and I am good at it!

I value my education because it prepares me for a bright future.

I manage my time efficiently to maximize learning.

I transform academic pressure into motivation.

I tackle every assignment eagerly and with dedication.

I conquer academic challenges with ease and confidence knowing that my hard work will lead to success.

I stay focused and attentive in class, soaking up knowledge like a sponge.

I appreciate the friends I've made at school and value each connection.

I believe in my ability to learn and understand new ideas.

I am excited about the chance to be creative and express myself in my education.

I am open to learning from all my experiences, both successes and challenges.

I am a problem solver who faces challenges with a positive mindset.

I eagerly explore my interests and discover my passions.

I am a lifelong learner who finds joy in the pursuit of knowledge.

I am a good friend who nurtures positive relationships with my peers.

I am confident in expressing my thoughts and opinions, knowing that my voice matters.

I remain strong during tough times and keep a positive attitude.

I am motivated to succeed in all areas of my life.

I am confident in my academic abilities.

I am a kind and helpful classmate, making a positive impact in my school.

I am blessed to learn something new every day.

I am dedicated to continuous learning and growth.

I am an unstoppable force in my academic journey.

I am an academic superstar in the making.

DAY 3

Affirmations for Exam Success

The best way to overcome your fear of exams
is to prepare for them.
-Marian Wright

Recipe for success: Study while others are sleeping;
work while others are loafing; prepare while others
are playing; and dream while others are wishing.
-William A. Ward

I am becoming more confident with each day of study and preparation.

I am focused and determined. My study habits are helping me to achieve academic success.

I am consistent and dedicated to studying.

I am prepared with my study schedule, which is easy to stick to.

I am thankful for my capable and intelligent mind.

I am capable of excelling in my exams, and I will achieve the grades I desire.

I give myself more than enough time to prepare for my exams.

I feel good about myself and my preparations for my exams.

Every question I encounter is an opportunity to showcase my knowledge.

My memory is flawless when it comes to storing information for my exams.

When I feel overwhelmed by nerves, I take a moment to focus and breathe.

Each step of my preparation diminishes my fear.

I have positive coping mechanisms for stress.

I take time away from studying to relax and have fun.

I show myself patience and grace when I am preparing for my exams.

I will be fully prepared for my exams with the right study resources.

I am motivated and dedicated to my studies. Success is my choice.

I am an excellent student and work hard to enhance my future.

I am focused. I am prepared, and I am going to do exceptionally well today.

My memory is sharp and ready to take these exams.

Learning brings joy as I gain knowledge and understanding every day.

I let go of all worry and anxiety and embrace relaxation and focus.

I can solve any problem or challenge because I am a solution-finder.

The more I study, the better I become.

Exams are a great measure of my knowledge.

Good study habits are ingrained in me.

My loved ones are happy to help me study and prepare when needed.

Each test refreshes my ability to understand and process knowledge.

I release the need for perfection and accept my best.

My mind is clear, and I am ready to concentrate.

Preparation is the key to unlocking my full potential.

Focusing on my studies becomes easier every day.

I am detail-oriented, especially during exams.

I am brilliant and intelligent, and my memory is amazing.

I release my fears and open my mind to new information to pass my exams.

My worth is not defined by my grades.

When I spend time preparing I can tell myself I am doing my best.

I prioritize self-care in the lead-up to my exams.

I take breaks in between studying to give my brain a rest.

I celebrate progress, not just perfect scores.

I am a capable student and lifelong learner.

I am well supported by my teachers and loved ones.

I study with determination to build a brighter future.

I study hard so I can play harder.

DAY 4

Affirmations for Athletic and Extracurricular Achievement

If your teacher, coach, or mentor believes
you can do something, you're more likely to do it.
-Gwen Moran

Talent wins games, but teamwork
and intelligence win championships.
-Michael Jordan

I am a force to be reckoned with.

I am a trailblazer in my sport.

I am always improving and getting better.

I am a legend in the making.

I am practicing every day.

I am an asset to my team, and I help us succeed.

I am confident in my skills and abilities.

My mental toughness is unbreakable.

My technique is sharp, allowing me to perform at my peak even under the pressure of competition.

My stamina is constantly increasing.

I push myself to become the best I can be.

I listen to my hunger signs and fuel my body.

I am a leader on and off the field/court.

I am open to constructive feedback and always adaptable and coachable.

I am grateful for the support of my coach, teammates, and loved ones.

I am thankful for the opportunities my sport/activity has given me.

I cultivate my musical and artistic abilities through extracurricular activities.

I am dedicated to my sport and to being an inspiration to others.

I am a winner and have a winning mindset.

I am mentally tough and fearless in challenges.

I have no trouble finding motivation when training.

By practicing consistently, I am becoming the best version of myself.

I enjoy exploring new extracurricular activities.

I will keep pushing and striving for greatness.

I can stay focused and determined under pressure.

I never give up. I will surpass my expectations.

I am focused, disciplined, and ready to do my best.

I eat healthy foods and keep my body in top condition.

My potential is limitless, and my focus is laser-sharp.

I am a comeback kid with unwavering determination.

I am grateful for my body and what it can do.

I am a team player and work well with others.

I am always prepared and ready for competition.

I am confident in my ability to perform under pressure making me a force to be reckoned with.

AFFIRMATIONS FOR ATHLETIC AND EXTRACURRICULAR ACHIEVEMENT

I can focus my mind when I need to concentrate.

I enjoy practicing because practicing makes improvement and brings me closer to mastery.

I will reach my full athletic potential.

No matter the obstacle or struggle, I will endure.

I am proud of myself for exercising regularly.

My determination is unstoppable.

My hustle is relentless.

No matter what my goal is, I can achieve it.

I am committed to my training.

I am determined to stop making excuses.

I rely on food to fuel my performance.

It's okay to take rest days to avoid overexercising.

It's not about being perfect. It's about giving my absolute best.

I am proud of my progress.

I am committed to working out and eating healthy.

I fuel my body to be strong.

My body is a temple, and I look after it every day.

Even as an athlete, nurturing my mental health is my top priority.

My mental health and well-being is as important as my physical performance.

I honor my mind and body by giving them the rest and care they need.

I am patient, and I know seeing results takes time.

No matter the outcome of my games, I am always a winner.

I am proud of my courage to try out for the team.

I am focused, positive, and always give my best.

I approach tryouts with a winning mindset.

I stay calm and composed, no matter the outcome.

I am resilient and bounce back from any setbacks.

I am capable and motivated, and extracurricular activities are a great way to explore my interests.

Joining a club allows me to meet like-minded people and build strong friendships.

Trying new activities helps me discover hidden talents and passions.

Extracurriculars push me outside my comfort zone and help me grow as a person.

Participating in activities makes me feel more connected to my school and community.

Participating in extracurricular activities will boost my confidence and sense of accomplishment.

Being a part of a team or club helps me develop valuable leadership and communication skills.

My extracurricular activities will enhance my college applications and open doors to new opportunities.

Exploring various activities helps me develop time management and organizational skills.

Having fun and expressing myself creatively are important, and extracurriculars allow me to do that.

When I step outside my comfort zone, I find courage knowing that my faith prepares me to succeed.

I give my all, trusting God to bless all my endeavors.

Affirmations to Level Up Your Spirit and Soul

DAY 5

Affirmations to Grow Spiritually

Spiritual growth consists most in the growth of the root, which is out of sight.
-Matthew Henry

Spiritual development is not an accomplishment but a way of life. It is an orientation that brings its own rewards, and what is important is the direction of one's motives.
-David R. Hawkins

I am fearfully and wonderfully made.

I am a child of God, and I am surrounded by His love.

I am with God, and God is always with me.

I delight in the Word of God, and I meditate on it day and night, allowing it to guide and transform my life.

My life is a wonderful gift, and I am worthy of God's promises.

My heart will not be troubled or afraid. God has given me peace.

God renews my strength, and I have the endurance to keep going.

I have faith in God, and He loves me unconditionally.

Through God's help, I walk in power, love, and self-discipline.

I yield myself to God's will.

I trust in God with all my heart and lean not on my own understanding, acknowledging Him in all my ways.

God generously gives me wisdom as I ask for it.

God's Word helps me develop morals and uphold ethical values.

God has created me uniquely, and He knows me by name.

God has created me for a purpose, and I will find and fulfill it.

The peace of God rules in my heart.

The love of God flows through me. I am His, and He is mine.

I cultivate a spirit of gratitude, giving thanks to God in all circumstances and recognizing His daily faithfulness and love.

I am thankful, and I accept God's goodness in my life.

I am open to all opportunities and blessings that God sends my way.

I am led by God and trust in His guidance and divine wisdom.

I am made strong by God, and I do not need to fear.

As I wait on God, my power is renewed.

As I seek God, He hears me and delivers me from all my fears.

AFFIRMATIONS TO GROW SPIRITUALLY

I am strong in Him and in His mighty power.

I am totally healed—physically, mentally, emotionally, and spiritually.

I release doubt and fear and trust fully in God.

I will fulfill the purpose that God has for my life.

I am a vessel of God's love, and I extend kindness, compassion, and forgiveness to others.

God is for me and doing a good work in me.

I can walk confidently today because God's love is for me.

God is fighting my battles, and I will be victorious.

God has my back, and I am strong because of Him.

I walk in miracles beyond my expectations.

I accept everything that God has to offer me.

I let go of fear and embrace God's will for my life knowing everything will work out according to His perfect will.

I humbly surrender my will to God's will, seeking His guidance and direction in every aspect of my life.

I choose to see my difficulties as opportunities to grow closer to God.

I choose faith over fear.

I practice forgiveness towards myself and others, freeing my heart from resentment and anger.

I surrender my anxieties and worries to God, knowing that He cares for me and will provide for my needs.

I have a sound mind and an obedient heart.

I reject thoughts of fear, doubt, and negativity, replacing them with the truth of God's promises.

I embrace the power of prayer, knowing that it has the ability to move mountains and bring about miracles.

My strength comes from God, and He helps me do the impossible.

My steps are ordered by God, and I believe He has a purpose and plan for every season of my life.

DAY 6

Affirmations to Embrace Your Identity

Be yourself; everyone else is already taken.
-Oscar Wilde

To be yourself in a world that is constantly trying to make you something else is the greatest accomplishment.
-Ralph Waldo Emerson

I am valuable and have much to offer.

I am attractive inside and out.

I am choosing to see how wonderful I truly am.

I am confident and comfortable in my own skin.

I am my most valuable asset, so I act accordingly.

I am exactly how I should be, so I embrace my physical appearance.

I was created perfectly just as I am.

I will not compare myself to others. I am my own unique person.

I only compare myself to myself, and I am becoming the best version of myself daily.

I am not trying to fit in, because I was born to stand out.

I am unique and special in my own way and there is no one else like me.

I am one of a kind, and I have many amazing qualities.

I am unique and special, and I have my own set of talents and abilities that make me who I am.

I let go of past feelings that no longer serve me.

I know my self-worth, and I will not settle for less than I deserve.

I am worthy of taking care of myself physically, emotionally, and mentally.

I will stay true to myself and my own values.

I was born for a purpose and with a purpose.

I release the confusion of the world and its attempt to define my identity.

I respect myself and my body. I do not have to compromise my morals for anyone.

Others cannot diminish who I am. I refuse to let anyone degrade my self-image.

I am attractive and perfect the way I am; no one can tell me otherwise.

I am an original. I am whole, and I am complete just the way I am.

I am dedicated to discovering who I am and how great I can become.

I am continually discovering new talents and abilities within me.

I am strong. I am capable. I am loved.

I am powerful. I am a leader. I am enough.

AFFIRMATIONS TO EMBRACE YOUR IDENTITY

I am brave. I am confident. I am unstoppable.

I am smart. I am creative. I am imaginative.

I am important. I am accepted. I am appreciated.

I am kind. I am helpful. I am thoughtful.

I am curious. I am adventurous. I am bold.

I am resilient. I am adaptable. I am a problem-solver.

I am in control of my own thoughts and emotions and choose to focus on positivity.

I forgive those who have harmed me in my past and peacefully detach from them.

I love and accept myself and focus on the positive aspects of myself.

I matter, and I will not pretend to be someone I'm not.

I am worthy of living a life filled with purpose, passion, and joy.

I am free from negative self-talk and self-judgment when I look in the mirror.

I let go of all negative thoughts and embrace new, positive ones today.

I accept myself and my flaws; they are what makes me who I am.

My self-worth and self-esteem are not determined by a number on a scale.

My self-worth and self-esteem are not determined by the opinion of others.

I am here, and I am now, and I am taking responsibility for my life.

I am who I want to be starting right now.

I am unique and significant and have been perfectly fashioned by God.

I celebrate that God made me in his image, and I am not a mistake.

God defines who I am and why I am here and reveals it to me.

My identity comes from God, and he is pleased with who I am, and that is enough.

DAY 7

Affirmations to Increase Self-Love, Self-Esteem, and Self-Worth

Your words have so much power. Every day,
if you tell yourself, 'I love you,' if you give yourself
one word of validation, it will change your mind.
-Ashley Graham

The strongest factor for success is self-esteem:
Believing you can do it, believing you deserve it,
and believing you will get it.
-John Assaraf

I am worthy of loving myself.

I am loved.

I am loving and lovable.

I love myself unconditionally.

I love and approve of myself.

I love myself. I love my body. I love my mind.

I love who I am inside and out.

I appreciate myself. I accept myself. I forgive myself.

I love myself more and more each passing day.

I am worthy.

I am creative.

I am strong.

I am wanted

I am enough.

I am attractive.

I am blessed.

I am my own hero.

I fearlessly follow my dreams.

I feel great about who I am.

I feel joyful to look at how far I've come.

I am unique and amazing.

I am worthy of happiness and love.

I am perfect just the way I am.

I am in control of myself, and I am in control of my life.

I am creative and flexible, and I go with the flow of life.

I am unaffected by the judgment of others.

I am proud of my accomplishments.

I am not the anxiety attacking me; I am not what fears tries to tell me I am.

I am becoming the best version of myself.

I am grateful for the amazing, wonderful things in my life.

I am worthy of all the abundance, love, and amazing experiences I want.

I am unlike anyone else, and that is my best gift.

I am so grateful for this life.

I am doing the best that I can.

I am a force that the world needs.

I am optimistic and positive.

I am courageous and outgoing.

My worth is not determined by others.

I am responsible. I am independent. I am capable.

I am capable of achieving everything I want.

I am confident and intelligent.

My life is amazing.

My life is abundant.

My life is a blessing.

My life is rewarding and filled with joy.

My life is full of fun, exciting adventures and next-level experiences.

My space and boundaries are important.

I have unlimited power.

I have unique ideas to share with the world.

I have the ability to choose joy today.

I have great potential that I tap into every day.

I have a special gift that the world needs—that the world deserves to see.

I trust myself.

I trust that things are going to work out for my good.

I am worthy of positive experiences and blessings.

I deserve to fill this space.

I deserve good things. I deserve happiness and joy.

I fully accept who I am, even as I better myself.

I release self-criticism and choose self-love.

I believe in myself and my abilities.

I treat myself with respect and honor.

I view myself through kind eyes.

I expect the best for myself.

I learn and grow every day.

I matter. My life matters.

I can achieve anything I put my mind to.

I naturally feel good about myself.

I easily forgive others.

I do my best every day.

I am becoming the best version of myself.

I know myself, and I honor my boundaries.

I promise to be kind to myself.

I choose to forgive myself rather than judge myself.

I don't need anyone else's approval to love myself.

I promise to be kind to myself because I deserve such kindness.

I accept and embrace myself for who I am.

I make a difference in the world.

I know others look up to me.

I appreciate that others love me for who I am.

I accept that others value my skills and knowledge.

It is in my power to choose happiness and love myself.

I believe in my ability to overcome setbacks.

I have the power to create the life I want.

I have everything I need to succeed.

I deserve to be successful.

I deserve everything good that comes to me.

I am worthy and my worth isn't affected by someone else's opinion.

I am good-looking, smart, and fun.

I am a valuable and important person.

There's absolutely nothing out of my reach.

Life is beautiful, and I am grateful for all I have.

I have many good qualities.

I have self-worth and inner beauty.

I have the power to be who I want to be.

I have limitless potential.

My voice and ideas are important.

My feelings and needs are important.

My self-worth doesn't depend on how others see me.

My failures do not define me; they simply help me grow and learn.

I respect myself, and others appreciate me.

I trust in my abilities.

I do not need to compare myself to others.

I forgive myself for things I have done in the past.

I follow my dreams no matter what.

I know who I am, and I release the thoughts that don't serve me.

I practice self-compassion when I make mistakes.

I like who I am and who I am becoming.

The love I give myself is reflected in all areas of my life.

The more I practice loving myself, the more lovable I become.

The only approval I need for self-esteem is my own.

I am proud of myself.

I am a unique gift to the world.

I am good enough.

I am good-looking, intelligent, and full of life.

I am right where I am supposed to be.

I am empowered to have the things I seek.

I am comfortable in my own skin.

I deserve to treat myself, just because.

I deserve the compliments that I receive.

I deserve love and happiness.

Everything is possible for me.

Nothing can stop me from achieving my dreams.

Nothing can stop me from believing in myself.

I love myself and all my flaws.

I love myself more and more each day.

I love and accept myself exactly as I am.

I love my personality, and as I learn and grow, I love it even more.

I am one-of-a-kind and no one can replace me.

I am supported and loved by others.

I believe in my ability to overcome setbacks.

I am surrounded by grace and positivity.

I am creative, strong, powerful, brave, and inspired.

My mind is filled with loving thoughts.

My life is a miracle, and I belong here.

I treat my body with love and care.

I don't have to be good at something to enjoy it.

I don't need to overthink this. I let go of things that are out of my control.

I am my own best friend.

I am brave and strong.

I am grateful for my life.

I am thankful for my body, mind, and spirit.

I am growing for myself.

I can achieve anything I want in life.

I can assert myself and stand up for myself and others.

I value the effort and work I put into all aspects of my life.

I accept myself unconditionally.

I prioritize myself and my needs.

I make time to care for myself.

I choose to view my life positively.

I let go of my past and live in the present.

DAY 8

Affirmations to Overcome Negative and Suicidal Thoughts

Once you replace negative thoughts with positive ones, you'll start having positive results.
-Willie Nelson

They can't rescue you if they don't know you need it. Ask for help to fight another day.
-Unknown

I am not my emotions or my thoughts.

I am strong in mind, body, and spirit.

I am enough, and that's all that matters.

I am enough. I don't need to be perfect.

I am filled with positivity.

I train my mind to think optimistically.

I am in full control of my life.

I can control my thoughts, so I choose positive ones.

I give myself room to fail.

I give myself room to heal.

I give myself room to grow.

I give myself room to succeed.

I give myself room to thrive.

I love and approve of myself.

I love myself despite my thoughts.

It's okay to seek assistance. I am not alone.

I have faith in myself and my abilities.

I have the power to make the right choices for me.

I have made it this far, and I won't stop now.

I can do difficult things.

I can make a real difference.

I refuse to believe my own excuses.

I abandon old habits and choose new, positive ones.

I abandon all toxic thoughts.

Nothing is impossible, and life is great.

The world is full of possibilities.

Life is worth living despite my pain and sadness.

Obstacles are now falling away easily.

Today is a clean slate.

I am confident in asking for and accepting help.

I give myself permission to be me.

I give myself permission to be human.

I am bigger than fear. Fear does not define me.

I am filled with positive actions.

I am not afraid of failures and hardships.

I am delighted and content to have this life.

I am positive and will remain positive about my life.

I am in charge of my life and my happiness.

I am here with a purpose.

AFFIRMATIONS TO OVERCOME NEGATIVE AND SUICIDAL THOUGHTS

I am a miracle in motion.

I am blessed to see today. Every day is a gift.

I will not replay situations in my mind that upset or hurt me.

I will not become angry over things I cannot control.

I will survive this.

I will overcome these obstacles in front of me.

I will wake up tomorrow and do the best I can.

I choose happiness over sadness.

I release things that no longer serve me.

I release all thoughts that don't help me.

I release all negative thoughts.

I release the need to replay situations in my mind.

Thoughts can be changed.

Every thought I think is creating my future so I choose positive ones.

Toxic thoughts have no place in my life.

The past is over.

This darkness won't last forever.

Bad days will not last long if I remain strong.

I am much more than what I think I am.

I am loved and appreciated.

I am a talented person, and the world needs a talented person like me.

I am a work in progress.

I am self-sufficient and optimistic.

I am proud that I have come so far.

I am proud of all the hard days I have survived.

I am strong and can overcome anything in life.

I am tough. I will not give up on my life.

I am at peace with imperfection.

I am more than what people think I am.

I welcome positivity into my life.

I welcome health and happiness.

Quitting on myself is not an option.

Quitting on my life is not an option.

I am not alone. Help is always available to me.

I deserve love, joy, and happiness.

I don't have to be productive to see value in myself.

I overcome all obstacles and challenges in my life.

I shine brighter after dark days.

I forgive myself for any past mistakes I have made.

I forgive myself and let go of shame and blame.

I forgive myself and set myself free.

I focus on ways I can help myself get better.

My possibilities and capabilities are endless.

My life is a gift and it keeps on giving.

The world is better with me in it.

I have made it through other challenges, and I will make it through this one.

My negative thoughts do not define me.

I deserve happiness and joy.

I am surrounded by positive and supportive people who freely give encouragement.

My self-worth is not dependent on external validation or approval.

I am confident in my ability to overcome challenges and emerge stronger and wiser.

I am enough and don't have to prove anything to anyone else.

It's okay to feel sad today because tomorrow is a fresh start.

I am overcoming bad memories one step at a time.

People love me, and I am worthy of their love.

My needs are important, and it's okay to ask for help.

The negative things my mind or others say about me are not true.

I have the necessary strength and resilience to overcome any obstacle.

I choose to believe in myself.

I choose to see the beauty in myself and others.

I am deserving of forgiveness and grace.

I am in control of my thoughts, and I choose to be positive instead of negative.

I forgive myself and release my worries to God.

I let go of impatience and trust in God's plan.

God loves me and wants what's best for me.

DAY 9

Affirmations to Become More Grateful and Thankful

When gratitude becomes your default setting, life changes.
-Nancy Leigh Demoss

When life is sweet, say thank you and celebrate.
And when life is bitter, say thank you and grow.
-Shauna Niequist

I am forever grateful.

I am grateful to be alive.

I am grateful for good health.

I am grateful for all the lessons I've learned.

I am grateful for what my mistakes have taught me.

I am grateful for the small steps I achieve each day.

I am grateful for who I am and everything I am capable of.

My day begins and ends with gratitude.

Each and every day, I count my blessings.

I live in a state of gratitude, and I am always thankful.

I am thankful for everything in my life.

I am thankful to have a loving family.

I am thankful for every person who believes in me.

I am thankful for every person who supports me in some way.

I am thankful for every opportunity that comes to me.

I am thankful for all the doors that have opened for me.

I am thankful for this new day and all that it brings.

I am thankful for all the lessons I have learned, and I'm ready to move forward.

I am thankful that with each experience I become a better version of myself.

I am eternally grateful for all of the blessings I have in my life.

I am deeply grateful for the freedoms I enjoy.

I walk daily with an attitude of gratitude.

I give myself permission to be thankful regardless of my circumstances or emotions.

Gratitude changes my focus to the good in my life.

I am grateful for all the things in my life that bring me joy and happiness.

I am grateful for life's challenges for helping me grow and become who I am.

I am grateful for the abundance in my life.

I am grateful for everything–the good and the bad–because it developed me.

I am grateful for all the wonderful people in my life.

I am grateful for a roof over my head and a warm bed to sleep in.

I am grateful for the people that cross my path daily.

AFFIRMATIONS TO BECOME MORE GRATEFUL AND THANKFUL

I am grateful for my success.

I am grateful for my senses of taste, vision, hearing, touch, and smell.

I am grateful for my body and the health I have.

I am grateful for my relationships and the love and connection we share.

I realize that every situation in life has a purpose, and I am thankful for it.

I am thankful to God for bringing to pass all the wonderful things in my life.

Affirmations to Level Up Your Attitude and Confidence

DAY 10

Affirmations to Believe in Yourself

Life has no limitations, except the ones you make.
-Les Brown

Believe in yourself! Have faith in your abilities!
Without a humble but reasonable confidence in your
own powers you cannot be successful or happy.
-Norman Vincent Peale

I am full of unlimited potential.

I am a strong and powerful person.

I am capable and confident.

I believe in myself and my ability to succeed.

I am ready for whatever the future holds.

I am releasing all my old fears.

I am great at what I do.

I am not my thoughts.

I am not my fears.

I am proud of myself for showing up.

I am safe. I am protected. I am loved.

I am not a prisoner of my mind. I control my day.

My challenges help me grow.

My gifts are unique and one-of-a-kind.

My thoughts are valuable.

My mistakes will not define me.

My contributions are meaningful, valued, and abundantly rewarded.

My voice and opinions are important.

My strength is greater than any struggle.

My body is my home, and I choose to build it up instead of tear it down.

I will be kind to myself.

I will not question myself.

I will not stop until I reach my goals.

I will accept whatever comes my way and overcome.

There are people in my corner who support me.

Every day I am creating a life I love.

Every day I nurture my body.

Every step I take gets me closer to my goals.

Every challenge is an opportunity to grow.

Every day is another chance to shine.

I am not my fears.

I am accepted here.

I am valuable.

I am trustworthy.

I am full of life.

I am allowed to take up space.

I am strong and resilient.

I am bigger than any obstacle.

I am allowed to be wherever I want to be.

I am grateful for how much I have grown.

I am grateful for all the good things in my life.

I am understanding of others and their circumstances.

I am abundant in kindness and love.

I am happy when I challenge myself.

I am completely supported, safe, and rooted in the present moment.

I can accomplish great things.

I can ask for and receive help from others.

I can face difficult challenges.

I can face every challenge.

I can express my true self.

I can achieve everything I want in life.

I choose to love myself exactly as I am.

I choose to not give in to fear.

I choose to be happy.

I choose courage over fear and peace over perfection.

I have the grace to love the broken parts of me and pursue healing.

I have unique and valuable gifts to offer the world.

I have the power to change my story.

I have the courage to be seen.

I am in complete control of my emotions.

I am bigger than my doubts.

I am bigger than my insecurities.

I am enough, just as I am.

I am confident in my physical appearance.

I am engaging and welcomed when I enter a room.

I am growing into who I am supposed to be.

I am surrounded by positive people.

I am surrounded by uplifting, supportive people who believe in me.

I am able to ask for and accept help when I need it.

I am healthy and full of life.

I am always worthy. I matter.

I am willing to learn, grow, and change.

I thrive in everything I do.

I rise above all my insecurities.

I strongly believe in myself.

I empower and encourage everyone I know.

I celebrate my progress each and every day.

I accept compliments from others.

I love myself completely, flaws and all.

I forgive myself for my mistakes.

I deserve peace and well-being.

I speak to myself with loving-kindness.

I release all doubts and insecurities about myself.

I release fear and welcome faith.

I embrace the new me and let go of the old me.

I have all the tools for success.

I have the potential to achieve my dreams.

I have the power to make an impact on the world.

I receive solutions to all my problems.

I may make mistakes, but I am not my mistakes.

Mistakes do not define me.

I am focused on my journey.

I show compassion for myself in all situations.

I bring light to those around me.

I do not have to be perfect. I just have to show up.

I feel comfortable with my thoughts and feelings.

I feel protected and validated.

I already have everything I need for success.

It is safe for me to be my authentic self.

It's okay to step out of my comfort zone.

Nobody can make me feel small.

Success and abundance are my birthright.

The world will value my contributions.

In the face of fear and uncertainty, I choose gratitude and trust.

No matter what, I am always worthy of love, kindness, and respect.

DAY 11

Affirmations to Increase Confidence

Self-confidence is a super power.
Once you start to believe in yourself, magic starts happening.
-Oscar Auliq-Ice

Optimism is the faith that leads to achievement.
Nothing can be done without hope and confidence.
-Helen Keller

I am a confident person.

I am confident in my uniqueness.

I'm secure in who I am now and confident in who I am becoming.

I am my best source of motivation.

I am braver than I think.

I am stronger than I feel.

I am stronger than my fears.

I am stronger than my doubts.

Confidence is available to me now.

Confidence is possible for me now.

Confidence is mine.

I have all the confidence I need to tackle the day.

I have unshakable faith.

I have everything I need for success.

Every day I become a better version of myself.

Every day I grow more confident.

Everything is possible.

I can overcome any challenges.

I can overcome every obstacle that comes my way.

I embody confidence.

I see myself walking confidently into every situation.

I look forward to the future.

I deserve to feel good about myself.

I radiate self-confidence.

I shine bright like a diamond.

I am strong, confident, and courageous.

I am the master of my thoughts.

I am not afraid of the unknown.

It's okay to leave my comfort zone.

When I set my mind on something, I won't stop until I reach it.

There is nothing I am afraid of.

It's okay to fail because that's the road to success.

All I need to succeed is within me.

My confidence grows stronger every day.

Nobody has the right to make me feel worthless.

I am worthy of being confident.

I am aware of my unique gift to the world and share it freely.

I am a good person who deserves to be treated with love and respect.

I am compassionate with others and myself.

The more I let go, the better I feel.

The more I choose to be confident, the more confident I become.

My confidence is at the next level.

I can achieve everything I want.

I let go of my insecurities.

I stand up for myself.

I will tackle the day ahead with confidence.

I handle stressful situations with confidence.

I release everything that doesn't serve me.

Challenges are opportunities to grow and improve.

What I want is already here or on its way.

There are no roadblocks I cannot overcome.

I am free of negative self-talk.

I am a positive person, aware of my full potential.

I am grateful for my journey and its lessons.

I am ready to step into the most confident version of myself.

I conquer all limiting beliefs.

My mood doesn't depend on other people's opinions.

I love to meet other people and make new friends.

I am creative and open to new solutions.

My happiness and well-being are important.

My confidence comes with practice.

I accept compliments easily.

I receive positive people into my life.

I make a difference by showing up every day and doing my best.

I fill my mind with positive thoughts.

I choose not to stay around negative people.

I don't have to waste time on people whose company I don't enjoy.

I believe in my abilities and express my true self with ease.

I am confident that God is on my side.

DAY 12

Affirmations to Resist Peer Pressure and Drug Use

Peer pressure is pressure you put on yourself to fit in.
-Jeff Moore

Your mind is your greatest treasure. Protect it from drugs and don't allow it to sabotage your story.
-Lou Jones

I am totally in charge of my life.

I am brave. I am smart, and I stand up for myself.

I am in control of my own life.

I am surrounded by people who love me and will help me.

I am strong enough to say "no" without feeling bad.

I am stronger than the temptation of drugs.

I am not my mistakes. I am at peace with who I am.

My life is a gift, and I will use this gift with confidence.

My strength is greater than any struggle.

My life is free of drugs and negative influences.

My self-worth and self-esteem are not tied to how much others like me.

I focus on my own values, not society's expectations.

I refuse to give up on myself.

I will only spend my time with positive and supportive people.

I respect my body and keep it free from drug usage.

I am the guardian of my personal boundaries.

I am worthy of happiness and worth it.

I am proud of myself for releasing the things that no longer serve me.

I am in control of my choices and stand up for what matters to me.

I am becoming a confident and strong person.

I find it easy to turn down drugs and stay away from those who have them.

I release the fear of disappointing others when I say "no."

I release the need for others' approval.

I trust myself to enforce my boundaries consistently.

I am not tempted at all by drugs.

I do not need drugs or alcohol to have fun.

No person, place, or thing has any power over me. I am free.

I am no longer bound by my struggles, but empowered by my choices.

I am ready to start a new chapter in my life.

I am adapting to a new and healthy lifestyle.

I am both responsible and accountable for my choices and behavior.

I am proud of myself and my recovery.

I am grateful for each day that I am addiction-free.

I am strong and capable of overcoming any obstacle in my way.

I am capable of healing and moving forward with my life.

I am capable of embracing my flaws and imperfections and loving myself anyway.

I am worthy of a life filled with meaning, purpose, and fulfillment.

I am deserving of a life free from addiction and all its negative consequences.

I am resilient and can bounce back from setbacks.

I am proud of the progress I've made, no matter how small.

I forgive myself for the mistakes I have made, and I learn from them.

I forgive myself for what I did under the influence.

My boundaries create space for healthier relationships.

I have like-minded friends who support healthy and positive living.

I am grateful for the opportunity to create a new and better life for myself.

I am grateful for the opportunity to connect with others who understand my struggles and support my recovery.

I am capable of transforming my past into a source of strength and resilience.

I am capable of letting go of the past and embracing a positive future.

I am strong enough to resist peer pressure and stay true to myself and my recovery.

I will be a better person today than I was yesterday.

Everything I do today leads to a better tomorrow.

I believe in myself, I respect myself and I will not give up on myself.

I believe with God's power I will take back my power to have a better life.

DAY 13

Affirmations to Overcome Fear

Everything you want is on the other side of fear.
-Jack Canfield

Thinking will not overcome fear but action will.
-W. Clement Stone

I am fearless.

I am courageous in all that I do.

I am always eager to try new things.

I am strong enough to overcome any fear in my life.

I easily go beyond the limitations of my ego.

I easily release all fear and worry.

I take action now.

I always take action without hesitation or fear.

I keep pushing until I succeed.

I accept challenges with enthusiasm and confidence.

I always succeed in spite of setbacks.

I breathe in confidence and breathe out all fear.

I choose to feel safe and secure at all times.

I commit myself to developing the highest level of fearlessness in my life.

I constantly strive to move beyond my fears.

I do the things I fear and take control of my life.

I face all my fears head on.

I let all worries and fears float away as I focus my mind on my strengths.

I am turning into someone who is naturally confident and fearless.

I push forward and leave every fear behind.

I put my fears into proper perspective and then continue with confidence.

I replace any thought of fear with faith.

I see my fears for what they are—lifeless thoughts that I no longer give power to.

I willingly release all fears and doubts as they arise.

I walk in love, power, and self-discipline.

I naturally persist when things get tough.

I face and conquer fear with swift, decisive action.

I feel totally at ease in front of a group of people.

I have all the strength I need to defeat my fears.

My dreams are much greater than my fears.

My mind is too full of optimism to harbor worries and fears.

Today, I give myself permission to be greater than my fears.

Today, I give myself permission to succeed in the face of doubt.

From now on, fear isn't an option.

I know that all is okay in my life.

I know that my future is secure.

I know that fear disappears when I do the thing I fear.

I know that my fears disappear when I act in spite of them.

I have a purpose and fear won't stop me from fulfilling it.

Every day I bravely expand my comfort zone.

Gaining strength from difficulty is something I do naturally and easily.

The more I face my fears, the weaker they become.

Being confident and courageous comes naturally to me.

Facing my fears empowers me to rise above them.

Fear is nothing more than an emotion, and I am greater than my emotions.

As I challenge my fears and doubts, I am strengthened and empowered.

As I challenge my fears, I release my need to dwell on them.

My faith in God empowers me to overcome any fear.

DAY 14

Affirmations to Overcome Bullying

You're braver than you believe, stronger than you seem,
and smarter than you think.
-A.A. Milne

Don't be afraid to speak up for yourself.
Even if your voice shakes, people will hear you.
-Samantha Reed

I am attractive, worthy, and loved.

I am valuable, wonderful, and special in my own way.

I am respected, cared for, and a good person.

I am enough, and I am amazing.

I am more than any negative words thrown my way.

I am stronger than any bully's words or actions.

I let go of toxic emotions and embrace positivity.

I let go of toxic friendships and relationships no matter how close we are.

I grow stronger and more resilient each day.

I embrace therapy/counseling as a tool for my well-being and healing.

I am not what has happened to me. I am healed and whole, ready to embrace what lies ahead.

I am rebuilding my self-confidence every day.

I am deserving of love, respect, and kindness.

I am above the scars left by bullying.

I am perfect and complete just the way I am.

I can reach out and ask for help.

I can be strong and take back my freedom.

I forgive myself for believing that it's my fault when I'm bullied.

I forgive myself for thinking I need to hold on to anger when I'm bullied.

I forgive myself for believing that no one loves me or wants to protect me.

I forgive myself for believing the bullying can't stop, because it will end now.

I am a warrior against bullying and its effects.

I am a warrior, defending my peace and joy.

I am a warrior, and I protect my well-being and life.

I am a champion, rising above every challenge.

I am a powerful force against all forms of negativity and bullying.

I am an unstoppable force of power and freedom.

I am redefining my self-worth every day.

I am reclaiming my joy and peace one affirmation at a time.

I am continuously healing, and growing stronger each day.

I stand tall against any form of bullying.

I am worthy of a bully-free school and workplace.

I am empowered to seek support and speak up against bullying.

I am too big a gift to this world to feel self-pity.

I am enough and great just the way I am.

I am a great brother/sister/son/daughter.

I rise above depression with resilience and hope.

I will enjoy every moment, free from the shadows of bullying.

I remember my worth when faced with adversity.

I follow my dreams no matter the negative opinions of others.

I refuse to let bullying define my life story.

I embrace the therapy/counseling sessions that aid my healing.

I seek justice for wrongs, but also peace for my soul.

I forgive myself for those times when I have acted as a bully.

I forgive the bully for causing me emotional pain.

I forgive the bully for targeting me for reasons that had nothing to do with me.

I forgive those who stood by and did nothing while the bullying occurred.

I love and accept myself, even when I'm afraid I'll always face bullying.

I love and accept myself, even when I worry I'll never be 'cool' enough to avoid being bullied.

I love and accept myself, and I believe the bullying that occurred will stop forever.

I have the power to stand up for myself, and I am capable of handling any situation.

I am pushing beyond any limitations set by bullies.

I am healing from the hurts of the past.

I am overcoming anxiety with each passing day.

I am destined for greatness despite the obstacles.

I take responsibility for making the most of my life.

I get better every day in every way.

Attractiveness comes in all shapes and sizes, so I will not let anyone make me feel inferior or worthless.

I belong, and I am good enough.

Despite challenges, I press on, believing in myself and the value of my life.

My opinions matter, my emotions are valid, and I will not be silenced.

I am worthy of respect, and my voice deserves to be heard.

I matter, and what I offer this world also matters.

My self-worth is not determined by how others treat me.

I deserve to live a happy and fulfilling life, and I will not be denied.

I embrace God's love and healing power in my life.

I receive God's protection against those that mean me harm.

God is always with me, here to fight my battles.

Affirmations to Level Up Your Family and Friendships

DAY 15

Affirmations for Positive Parent and Family Relationships

> Love your parents. We are so busy growing up,
> we often forget they are also growing old.
> -Unknown

> What can you do to promote world peace?
> Go home and love your family.
> -Mother Teresa

I am a great son/daughter.

I am a responsible and caring son/daughter.

I am a loving and understanding son/daughter.

I am grateful for my wonderful family.

I am grateful for all members of my family, whether biological parents, grandparents, step-parents, foster or adoptive parents.

I am loved regardless of what my family looks like.

I am grateful for the time I get to spend with my family creating memories.

I am sensitive to the needs of my family.

I am a great role model to my family.

I treat my parent(s) with love and respect.

I treat my parent(s) with patience and kindness.

I know how to communicate positively with my mother and/or father.

When I lose my temper, I own up and apologize.

When I am wrong, I say I am sorry.

I take responsibility for my actions, and I'm quick to apologize.

I will avoid blaming others and take responsibility for my own actions.

Even though I make mistakes, my family still loves me.

Since I can't always tell what they're thinking, I directly ask my parent(s) for better understanding.

Since my parent(s) can't read my mind, I respectfully share what I am thinking and feeling with them.

There is peace and love in my home, no matter how chaotic it feels.

I will always show my family how much I love them through my words and actions.

My family and I completely support each other in all our endeavors.

I love my family with all my heart.

I love to help my mother and/or father in any way I can.

I love bringing joy into the lives of my family.

I love looking for ways to make my mother's and/or father's life easier.

I hug my mother and/or father and sibling(s) daily.

Sometimes my parents/siblings feel sad or angry, and that's okay.

My parent(s) and I are both learning, and sometimes that is hard.

I don't know everything, and that is okay.

I make mistakes, and that is okay.

Sometimes I feel frustrated, and that is okay.

I can't control the issues in my family, but I can control my reactions.

I let go of what can't be changed and release fear and anger, making space for peace.

I learn how to take breaks and breathe when I am stressed out.

My family accepts me exactly as I am.

I have a great relationship with my mother and/or father and sibling(s).

I enjoy helping my sibling(s) when they ask.

I set a positive example for my sibling(s).

I look after my sibling(s) to the best of my ability.

I encourage my sibling(s) to have big dreams.

I respond to my siblings with patience and love.

I feel loved and respected by my family.

I respect my siblings and mother and/or father.

I release any past negative situations with my family and work towards building a better future together.

It's okay to seek out extra help and support when I need it.

I am considerate and respectful of the feelings of everyone in my family.

I am not afraid to tell my family when they've upset or disappointed me.

I have boundaries, and I will ask my family to respect them.

I always pay close attention to what my mother and/or father says.

I am peaceful when speaking with family members.

I demonstrate my love for my family in many ways.

I love making my parent(s) lives more enjoyable.

I love spending time with my sibling(s).

I love taking care of my family and home.

I only speak loving words to my family.

I respect my parent(s) need for privacy.

We depend on and support each other in tough times.

We work together to become strong and happy.

We create a safe place for honest communication.

Every person in our family brings unique strengths, making us stronger together.

My family is a safe place for everyone.

My family has unlimited potential.

My family is important and special to me, and I tell them so often.

I inspire my sibling(s) to be the best they can be.

I teach my sibling(s) how to use empowering affirmations, boosting their confidence.

I strive to be the best son/daughter that I can possibly be.

I am a blessing to my family.

I speak encouraging words into each and every member of my family.

We laugh together, pray together, and celebrate each other.

My family has healthy, strong, and loving relationships.

My family is whole, healthy, and walking in the fullness of our purposes.

My family builds each other up, and does not tear each other down.

My family is blessed and loved by God.

DAY 16

Affirmations for Healthy Friendships

The best vitamin for making friends is B1.
-Suzanne Woods Fisher

True friends are never apart,
maybe in distance but never in heart.
-Helen Keller

I am worthy of positive friendships.

I am open to lasting friendships.

I am open to new friendships who share my values.

I am grateful for the wonderful friends in my life.

I am free to be myself with my friends.

I am a good friend, and I treat others with kindness and respect.

I am surrounded by friends who inspire me to be my best self.

I am a great friend who is always there when needed.

My friends always have my back, and I have theirs.

My friends love being around me, and I love being around them.

My friends are always there to encourage me.

My friends love me just as I am, and I love them as they are.

Being lovable around others requires loving and appreciating myself first.

I choose to surround myself with people who elevate me and not tear me down.

When someone shows me who they are, I listen.

My friends honor and respect my values.

My friends have good values.

My friends are enjoyable and positive.

My friends make me laugh, and that gives me joy.

My best friends make the best company.

Any toxic people in my life are better left behind.

I don't need a lot of friends, just the right ones.

I have the right to choose friendships that benefit me and not hinder me.

I can be honest with my friends, just like they're always honest with me.

I am always striving to be a supportive friend.

I am grateful for the people I have in my life.

I am surrounded by the love of my friends.

I am an exceptional friend, always treating others with compassion, empathy, and respect.

I appreciate my friends for their smarts and talents.

It is okay to be different from my friends.

I do not have to fit in to belong or to be important.

My friendships are built on trust and understanding.

My friends accept me for who I am.

My friends believe in me and support my dreams.

I am a positive influence on my friends' lives.

I am open to forming meaningful connections with new people.

I am open to genuine and lasting friendships.

I am not willing to compromise my beliefs or values for a friendship.

I can say no to friends, and they'll understand.

I will not use harmful words or spread rumors when I have conflicts with my friends.

I choose to release negativity and focus on fostering positive friendships.

I forgive and let go of any past misunderstandings with my friends.

I let go of any jealousy towards my friends.

I choose to let go of friendships that are disrespectful and unwise.

I release any friendships that are not healthy and safe.

Letting go of negativity is self-care.

Being sad about losing a friendship is totally normal.

I allow myself to mourn any lost friendships, and I'm grateful for the lessons learned.

I am grateful to have overcome hurdles with my friends. We've grown closer and stronger together.

I am grateful that my friends respect my boundaries.

I support and encourage my friends and our differences make us powerful.

I release the insecurities holding me back from making new friends.

I see every day as an opportunity to make new friends.

I enjoy getting to know new people.

I'm ready to welcome supportive people into my life.

I have healthy boundaries with my friendship circle.

I'm warm, kind, and compassionate around my new friends.

My friends support and care for me through the ups and downs.

My friends and I encourage one another in all our life goals.

My friends and I celebrate each other's successes and provide support during challenges.

My friends and I motivate each other to pursue meaningful goals.

I look for friends who empower me, and I strive to do the same to them.

I am open to like-minded people entering my life.

Instead of isolating myself, I'll actively seek out friendships with people who share my values.

I am blessed with an abundance of loving friends.

I am blessed to have friends who truly care about my well-being.

I trust God to guide me to the right friends.

DAY 17

Affirmations for Dating and a Future Spouse

A healthy relationship will never require you to sacrifice your friends, your dreams, or your dignity.
-Dinkar Kalotra

Love shouldn't make you less. Love should make you more. More of who you are. More confident. More brave.
-Angela Bassett

I am worthy of a healthy, loving relationship.

I am worthy of my future spouse's love and respect.

I am important, worthy, and loved even if I'm not in a dating relationship.

I am full of happiness and joy regardless of my relationship status.

I am amazing and the right person will see my value.

I am enough. I am strong and attractive inside and out.

I am worth the wait and so much more.

I am content, hopeful, and free from anxiety about finding my future spouse.

I am becoming the best version of myself by pursuing my education and career before a relationship.

I am not defined by my relationship status.

I will not settle for less than what's best for me.

The right person will appreciate my uniqueness and creativity.

My past does not define me and will not hinder my future relationship.

My love life will be a reflection of the love I have for myself.

I love who I am, and so will my future spouse.

I am capable of being in a fulfilling, healthy and whole relationship.

I say goodbye to the wrong relationship and say hello to true love.

I am getting prepared for an amazing relationship by pursuing my purpose and educating myself.

I am worthy of love, care, and understanding.

I am worthy of a future spouse who cherishes me for who I am.

I am a positive influence on those around me.

I am surrounded by people who respect, honor and value me.

I am letting go of any fears of failure in finding the right person.

When someone has a crush on me, I treat them with respect and kindness.

If someone I have a crush on doesn't want to get to know me better, I'll still be kind and respectful.

With my parents' permission to date, I will only date those who respect my boundaries and values.

I will listen to the advice of my parents when it comes to dating and a future spouse.

I will be accountable to my parents/family/guardians when it comes to a relationship.

I will not allow dating to become a distraction from the pursuit of my purpose and education.

I create and stick to boundaries in my relationship.

Dating and courtship will be a joyful experience for me.

My dating life doesn't define my self-worth.

My value comes from who I am, not just my physical body.

Every dating experience helps me learn more about myself and what I want.

I am comfortable saying no if something doesn't feel right.

It's okay to set boundaries and expectations.

Breakups are a normal part of dating, and it doesn't define my worth.

I learn from each experience and become stronger.

I am proud of who I am becoming and will always be responsible and accountable for my actions.

I will be a great blessing to my future spouse.

I will feel comfortable sharing my feelings and thoughts with my future spouse.

I will feel free to be myself with my future spouse.

I will feel loved and cherished in my relationship.

I will communicate in a healthy and loving way.

Loving myself first allows me to truly love my future spouse.

My future spouse will come into my life at the right time.

My spouse will value me and love me for who I am.

My spouse will treasure me and protect me.

My spouse will be faithful to me and give of their time, treasure, heart, and attention.

My spouse will make me feel loved and safe.

My spouse will trust and respect me.

My spouse and I will be perfectly matched.

My spouse and I will support each other to become successful individuals.

My spouse and I will share a strong and healthy love for each other.

My spouse and I will resolve our conflicts respectfully and peacefully.

My spouse and I will be generous with one another.

My spouse and I will think the best of one another.

My spouse and I communicate effectively, truthfully, and openly.

My spouse accepts my flaws and helps me to become a better version of me.

I am preparing myself emotionally and mentally for a successful marriage.

I am creating a love story that will honor my parents and honor God.

I date/court confidently knowing that God cares for me and has my back.

I open my heart to God's love and trust that my mate's love will follow.

I trust God to help me find true love at the right time, because he knows best.

I trust God to lead me to my future spouse who shares my values and strengthens my faith.

DAY 18

Affirmations for Healing a Broken Home

> There is always hope. Even when the skies are grey,
> the sun is still shining above the clouds.
> -C.S. Lewis

> Your inner peace is the greatest and most
> valuable treasure that you can discover.
> -Vincent van Gogh

I am capable of finding peace in chaos.

I am stronger than the tough times in my home.

I am strong enough to get through this.

I am worthy of happiness.

I am thankful to see another day.

I am letting go of what has broken my heart to find healing and peace.

I am healed from all family trauma.

Relationships in my family that have been broken are being restored.

It is okay to have healthy family boundaries.

We are willing to meet together, listen to each other's point of view, and freely discuss differences in order to resolve conflict.

I walk in forgiveness and release what is outside of my control.

It is okay to get therapy to deal with family relationships that need repair.

I can accept when a relationship is broken or ended; it is okay to grieve and have healthy boundaries.

I can move past hurtful things from my past and have hope for the future.

Just because I'm raised in a broken home doesn't mean I'm broken.

Just because I'm raised in a broken home doesn't mean I'm worthless.

The choices others in my family make do not define me.

I courageously move forward and embrace my healing journey.

I am surrounded by positive and supportive examples even if they are outside of my family.

I never lose hope that better days are ahead.

My home is my refuge and safe place.

My home is full of joy, peace, and love.

My feelings and my life matter.

My family may have struggles, but we always support each other through the tough times.

I use kind words in my home and about my home.

If my parents are not able to see me, I will see myself.

I am loved and accepted just as I am.

Taking care of my own needs is responsible, not selfish, allowing me to better support others.

I don't need drugs or alcohol to cope with stress or family challenges.

I let go of all worries that drain my energy.

I have people that care about me and are willing to help me.

I love myself unconditionally.

I am loved and appreciated.

Today I will release stress and embrace peace.

Today I prioritize my peace of mind and self-care.

Today is going to be a great day.

I recognize painful moments, but I know it will pass and brighter days are ahead.

I give myself permission to heal.

I can be gentle with myself as I heal.

My anxiety is temporary, and I let it go.

I am letting go of fear and stress.

I am free from the mistakes and baggage of my past.

I am safe, at peace, and protected.

I am in control of my peace.

I will take the time to care for my needs today.

I only need to take one step at a time.

It's okay for me to find joy even while I'm in pain.

I take comfort in the memories of my loved one.

I allow myself to feel my grief and then let go.

I will hold on to love and release the grief.

Grief has no timeline, so I will be gentle and patient with myself.

The sorrow I feel from my loss is temporary; things will get better.

Quitting on myself is not an option.

I can and I will heal.

I choose peace over perfection.

I choose progress over perfection.

This is not my forever. While my home may be broken now, I have the power to create a brighter future for myself.

In the midst of a difficult situation, I prioritize my own well-being.

I am worthy of self-care and taking care of my mental and emotional health.

I let go of what I cannot control.

I forgive myself and others for past mistakes.

I choose to respond with calmness and love.

I find peace in every situation.

Even when the road gets bumpy, I hold onto the belief that things will work out.

Together, we are stronger than any family problem, and we can overcome anything.

We stand together, no matter what happens, and we will always be there for each other.

My home will be filled with love and laughter. Anxiety has no place here.

My home is full of possibilities and wonderful memories will be made here.

My family is strengthened by faith, believing our prayers are heard.

Affirmations to Level Up Your Health and Wellness

DAY 19

Affirmations for Health, Healing, and Wellness

A healthy outside starts with a healthy inside.
-Robert Urich

Happiness is an inside job. Don't assign anyone else that much power over your life.
-Mandy Hale

I am healed.

I am in great shape and continue to do the work to be so.

I am treating my body as a temple.

I am worthy, talented, deserving, and healthy.

I am healed of all heartbreaks and disappointments.

I do not hold grudges.

I let go of things that I cannot control.

I am healed of all emotional pain I feel.

I say yes to all things that support good healthy living.

I say no to things that do not serve me or my health.

I daily consume fresh, nourishing food from nature.

I love and care for my body.

I love myself unconditionally.

I love everything that has made me who I am.

I am worthy of all things wonderful.

I am worthy of good health.

I am allowed to feel good about myself.

I am not the negative thoughts that come to my mind.

I am getting healthier every day.

I am active.

I am thriving.

I am not a victim.

I am optimistic and secure.

I am at peace with everyone including myself.

My health and healing are my top priority.

My past does not define my present or my future.

My hardships bring me opportunities.

My life is a beautiful gift, and I respect it.

I allow myself to heal inside and out.

I overcome sad moments and bad days.

I release all emotional baggage.

I take time out for my mental health and sanity.

I create space to heal my broken heart and let go of the past.

I am thriving in my healing journey.

I am healthy and strong in my spirit, soul, and body.

I am healthy and wise and listen to the advice of my doctors.

I see myself as fully healthy, and I take action to be so.

AFFIRMATIONS FOR HEALTH, HEALING, AND WELLNESS

My immune system is healthy and strong.

I am healed of all sickness, illness, and disease.

Water is good and gives life to my body.

Sunshine supports my health.

I get plenty of rest, and I sleep well.

I wake up rejuvenated and strong.

I prioritize exercise and physical fitness.

My muscles give me the support I need.

I have a healthy and pain-free body.

All my systems function perfectly—skeletal, muscular, nervous, circulatory, respiratory, digestive, urinary, and lymphatic.

I see myself at my highest and healthiest potential, and I am focused to get there.

I choose to be happy.

I am grateful for who I am and can be.

I am thankful to be alive today.

I am falling in love with taking care of myself.

I have a healthy body and a brilliant mind.

I deserve peace and mental well-being.

I accept my imperfections.

I feel loved and live in peace.

I give myself permission to heal.

I express my feelings respectfully.

I allow myself to rest when my body needs it.

I allow myself to give and receive love.

I treat myself with respect daily.

My life is filled with health and happiness.

There is no room for drama in my life.

The more I let go, the more freedom and healing I have.

DAY 20

Affirmations for Physical Purity

Abstinence is not a sign of weakness,
but a display of incredible strength.
-Robert South

Waiting is a sign of true love and patience. Anyone can say
'I love you,' but not everyone can wait and prove it's true.
-Unknown

I am confident and comfortable in my own skin.

I am confident in my ability to resist temptation.

I am in control of my body and my choices.

I am empowered to set healthy boundaries and protect myself.

I am not missing out on anything by saving my body for marriage.

I am creating a future full of love, joy, and happiness.

I am good-looking and love every part of myself, inside and out, just as I am.

I am more than my appearance; my body is an instrument, not an ornament.

I am at peace with my appearance and respect my body as a sacred temple.

My physical purity is a sacred part of me, and I treat it with respect.

My values guide my choices, and I stay true to them.

My values are my compass, guiding me towards healthy choices.

My future spouse will appreciate and be honored by my choices.

Every choice I make reflects the conviction and integrity I hold within.

Physical purity is a form of self-care and self-love.

I have the power to set boundaries and say no.

Saying "no" is a sign of strength and self-respect.

My choices are valid and deserve to be respected.

I find strength and inspiration from others who share my values.

I know I am not alone in choosing physical purity.

I choose joy and happiness in every area of my life.

Physical purity does not limit my happiness, it enriches it.

Physical purity allows me to focus on my passions and personal goals.

Physical purity allows me to focus on developing emotional maturity.

I honor myself by living in accordance with values and beliefs.

I am building a life that is authentic and true to who I am.

I am building a foundation for a fulfilling, strong and loving relationship.

I am attractive in my own way and refuse to let social media dictate how I feel about myself.

I am worthy of love, respect and acceptance, from myself and others.

I am worthy of a love that aligns with my values.

I prioritize self-care and respect the body of others and myself.

I stand firm in my values and make choices that align with my beliefs, regardless of others' expectations.

I surround myself with people who support my physical and emotional well-being.

I make conscious choices that support my long-term physical health.

I will wait for the right person in marriage and it will be worth it.

I value my body as a temple to honor and hold sacred.

I don't need to compromise my values or integrity to please others.

Saying "no" allows me to wait for someone who truly loves, honors and respects me.

Choosing physical purity is an act of self-respect and empowerment.

Choosing physical purity allows me to invest my energy in myself, my pursuits and my well-being.

Love is expressed in many ways, not just physically.

I am not defined by people's standards; I define my worth, and I am priceless.

I am confident in who I am; peer pressure does not sway my decisions or diminish my self worth.

I am strong against peer pressure, finding strength in my faith and the courage to be myself.

I am a positive influence on my peers, leading by example, and encouraging others to stay true to their values.

I am empowered by the strength within me and willing to wait for my future spouse.

I set boundaries to protect my physical and emotional space.

My self-worth is defined by my values and beliefs, not by the approval of others around me.

I choose physical purity to protect my emotional well-being and ensure a relationship built on a foundation of genuine love, not temporary desires.

My inner strength empowers me to wait for a true love that truly deserves me.

My energy is precious, and I choose to nurture and protect it for my well-being and personal growth.

My emotional and spiritual well-being are important to me.

I choose to respect my body and honor God with physical purity.

DAY 21

Affirmations for Better Mental Health

Mental health problems don't define who you are.
They are something you experience. You walk in the rain
and you feel the rain, but you are not the rain.
-Matt Haig

Your mental health is a priority. Your happiness is essential.
Your self-care is a necessity.
-Unknown

I am mentally strong.

I am mentally well and stable.

I am choosing to focus on my mental wellness.

I am capable of overcoming my mental health challenges and leading a happy life.

I am not my diagnosis.

I am healing.

I am in control.

I am tougher than the things that make life tough.

I am more than my trauma.

My mental health diagnosis and the challenges I face do not define me.

My anxious thoughts do not define me.

I fill my mind with positive thoughts.

I love myself unconditionally.

I love and approve of myself.

I have the strength to survive this.

I have coping skills to get through this crisis.

I have the final say in all of my emotions.

I release all of my worries.

I release tension from my body.

I release myself from stress.

I release toxic and negative thoughts.

I choose to react positively to all situations.

I choose to focus on the good.

Better mental health is possible for me.

Healing is possible for me.

Every day I am becoming a better version of myself.

One setback doesn't undo all that I have learned and accomplished.

I am in the process of actively healing my mental health for good.

I am doing the best I can.

I am happy to be me.

I am not ashamed of having anxiety.

I am in control of my mind.

I am in control of my life.

I accept the things I cannot control.

I am freeing myself from stress.

I can reach out to people who love me and get the support I need.

My loved ones look forward to when I reach out to them.

I prioritize and practice self-care.

I treat myself with compassion, kindness, and love.

I give energy to my solutions, not my problems.

I will not stress over things I cannot control.

I will not let my worries about tomorrow steal my peace today.

I will think only positive thoughts today.

I am strong, confident, and courageous.

I am thankful for the positive things in my life.

I am loved, wanted, and strong.

I am loved, important, and unique.

I allow myself to only be in healthy friendships.

My life is filled with miracles. My life is the greatest miracle of all.

I love what I see when I look in the mirror.

I love myself for who I am.

How I feel matters.

I deserve happiness.

I embrace my imperfections and love myself unconditionally.

I take time to care for my spirit, soul, and body.

I value and prioritize my mental health as much as my physical health.

I can overcome anything with patience and practice.

I care about my mental health, and I am willing to put it before productivity.

I care for myself daily.

I believe in my ability to get through this.

I accept my flaws and find beauty within them.

There are people out there who will help me.

Reaching out for support is an act of strength.

I feel calm, safe, and peaceful inside.

This situation is challenging, but I will overcome it.

I face anxiety with courage and strength.

Anxiety is not who I am, and it does not control my life.

Depression is not who I am, and it does not control my life.

I control my thoughts—they don't control me.

I can overcome any stressful situation.

The panic and discomfort I feel are only temporary.

I take a deep breath, smile, and start again.

I am a child of God. My life is whole and complete.

DAY 22

Affirmations for Overcoming Depression

The best cure for worry, depression, melancholy, brooding,
is to go deliberately forth and try to lift with one's sympathy
the gloom of somebody else.
-Arnold Bennett

Sometimes, life will kick you around, but sooner or later,
you realize you're not just a survivor. You're a warrior,
and you're stronger than anything life throws your way.
-Brooke Davis

I am not my depression.

I am gaining strength every single day.

I am enough, and that is all that counts.

I am worth the time it will take to heal within.

I am a work in progress, and that's okay.

I am loved and appreciated even when it doesn't seem like it.

I am not less of a person because of how I feel.

I am much more than what I think I am.

I am not alone in this.

I can have a new beginning.

I can take this one day at a time.

I can overcome this moment and have a good day.

I can challenge negative thoughts with positive ones.

My life is beautiful.

My future is bright.

My feelings are real, but they don't define me.

My life has meaning.

I will gain strength every single day.

I will become a healthy and strong person.

I will experience joy and happiness again.

I will learn and grow through this difficulty.

I give myself permission to be free.

I give myself time to heal.

I trust in myself to continue to hope.

I am loved despite my sadness.

I am stronger than I realize.

I am needed regardless of how I feel.

I am valuable regardless of how I feel.

I am surrounded by love and support.

I am more than my trauma.

I am not broken.

I am not to blame for my depression.

I am capable of feeling good, positive, and content.

I am grateful to be alive.

I am here for a reason and a lifetime.

This discomfort won't last forever.

This feeling won't last forever.

This is only temporary.

These thoughts and feelings do not define me.

This sadness and depression does not define me.

This crisis will pass, and I will be okay.

I am resilient.

I am in the process of positive change.

I am worthy of happiness.

I am whole and complete.

I am not perfect, and that's okay.

I am more than my opinions of myself.

I am valued even when I'm not productive.

I am more than my depression.

I am in charge of how I feel, and today, I am choosing happiness.

I am learning more about how to handle my depression every day.

There is nothing wrong with me because I feel sad.

I'll have a great day today.

Life is an amazing gift.

It's okay to ask for help.

Asking for help with depression is how I show myself love.

Depression does not mean I am not loved or loving.

Depression is just a human condition, and I am only human.

Depression does not have the final word. I will be free.

I have made it this far, and I will not stop.

I have many gifts and talents.

I have many positive things in my life.

Nourishing myself is my top priority.

I love and accept myself unconditionally, especially on days like this.

I appreciate my life.

I value and respect myself.

I love my imperfections.

I forgive myself, and I don't blame myself.

I do my very best, and that's enough.

I take care of myself even when it's difficult.

I take another step toward positive change every day.

Every situation gives me an opportunity to learn and grow.

Every day is a gift, and I am blessed to see today.

I have God's strength in my weakness.

I trust in God to overcome this depression.

DAY 23

Affirmations for Improving Your Body Image

You have been criticizing yourself for years and it hasn't worked.
Try approving of yourself and see what happens.
-Louise Hay

Empower yourself by refusing to let your mind bully your body;
instead, nurture it with positive words.
-Lou Jones

I am gorgeous inside and out.

I am worthy inside and out.

I am attractive just as I am.

I am perfect and complete just the way I am.

I am worth celebrating.

My body is my home, and I choose to build it up instead of tearing it down.

My body is a gift. I treat it with love and respect.

My body is my best friend.

My body is wonderful, just as it is.

My body is a vessel for my awesomeness.

I love my body.

I love everything about my body.

I love how I look.

I love my teeth and my smile.

I love my strong hands and feet.

I love my hair just the way it is.

I love my waistline and shape.

I love my body at every stage of its journey.

I love me.

I don't need validation from others.

I feel attractive in my skin.

I feel confident in my skin.

I do not compare my body to others.

I support others in their pursuit to feel positive about their body.

I accept all of me with love.

I strive to be healthy at any size.

I accept who I am, and I will not be defined by my weight or size.

I am open to loving my body just as it is.

I am defined by who I am inside, not how I look.

I give myself permission to feel and look attractive.

I treat my body with care and love.

I choose to think positively about myself.

I choose to love myself exactly as I am.

I like the person I am right now.

I have a loving relationship with my body.

I have no need to put anyone down to elevate myself.

I have no need to compare myself to magazine photos, which are airbrushed, photoshopped, and distorted.

AFFIRMATIONS FOR IMPROVING YOUR BODY IMAGE

I have the power to change anything I want.

I am allowed to take care of myself.

My body is a masterpiece.

My body supports me every day.

My body does not determine my worth.

I choose progress over perfection.

My very existence makes the world a better place.

My differences are what make me, me.

I take my own power back.

My mind is a friend to my body, not a bully.

I honor my body.

It feels good to take care of my body.

Food doesn't have to be the enemy; it can be nurturing and healing.

This body makes things happen; this body is strong.

Other people's opinions about my body are irrelevant.

Being skinny or a certain body size is not my identity. I am defined by who I am on the inside.

I deserve to love my body today, not only after I reach my ideal weight.

No one has the power to make me feel bad about myself without my permission.

Loving my body is a demonstration of power.

There is more to life than worrying about my weight.

I will always treat my body with the love, care, and appreciation it deserves.

My changing body does not determine my confidence—how I feel does.

I am becoming the best version of myself.

I feel safe in my body.

Today, and every day, I am blessed.

I don't compare myself to others. Comparison is the thief of joy.

I don't compare myself to others. Comparison is the enemy of my progress.

I don't compare myself to others. I'm on my own unique journey.

I don't compare myself to others. I'm busy working on myself.

I don't compare myself to others. I will shine like the sun in my due time.

I don't compare myself to others. I find complete satisfaction within.

I look exactly the way I'm supposed to because I was created in God's image.

Affirmations to Level Up Your Success and Future

DAY 24

Affirmations for Developing a Success Mindset

To change your life, you have to change yourself.
To change yourself, you have to change your mindset.
-Wilson Kanadi

Your life is as good as your mindset.
-Unknown

I am worthy of success.

I am intelligent, insightful, and wise.

I am skillful, talented, and gifted.

I am strong, brave, and confident.

I am capable of achieving greatness.

I am open to limitless possibilities.

I choose to embrace the best version of myself.

I choose faith over fear.

I say yes to new opportunities.

I envision a prosperous future for myself.

I don't just seek opportunities, I create them.

I have everything I need to be successful.

I turn failures into stepping stones and setbacks into comebacks.

I was born to do great things.

I don't need anyone's permission to be successful.

My great work ethic will be rewarded.

My thoughts are free of self-imposed limitations.

My mind is laser-focused on hitting my daily, weekly and monthly goals.

My income is always increasing.

My financial future is full and fruitful.

I achieve whatever I set my mind to.

I pursue my goals relentlessly until they are obtained.

I believe in my ability to be successful.

I have the power to transform my life.

I overcome all obstacles and challenges that stand between me and success.

I have the right mentors to help me achieve my success aspirations.

I am smart. All my ideas bring profit.

I am my best source of motivation.

I see opportunities everywhere.

I am developing a detailed plan to achieve my goals.

I am willing to do whatever it takes to increase my income and succeed.

I am proud of myself and all that I have accomplished.

I am open to becoming a successful entrepreneur.

I am more than my mistakes.

I am at peace with who I am.

I am creating a life I love.

I am relentless in the pursuit of success.

I am highly motivated and productive.

I take charge of my financial situation.

I spend less than I earn.

I give myself permission to prosper.

I release all negative thoughts and mindsets about wealth and prosperity.

I have the ability to reach all my personal and financial goals.

I welcome success in all areas of my life.

I find it easy to believe in myself.

I have a positive attitude, and I never quit.

I celebrate my own success and the success of others.

I will leave a legacy for my family.

Working smarter, not harder, comes naturally to me.

My progress is getting me closer to where I want to be.

Every day, in every way, I am becoming a better version of myself.

Being successful is my birthright.

DAY 25

Affirmations for Achieving Your Goals

We all have big dreams, high hopes, and grand plans. You are chosen to do great, big, world-changing, culture-shattering, life-giving, audacious things. The problem is most of us get tricked out of starting small. The truth is– the bigger the dream, sometimes, the smaller the start.
-Ruth Jones

A dream written down with a date becomes a goal.
A goal broken down into steps becomes a plan.
A plan backed by action makes your dreams come true.
-Greg Reid

I am capable of achieving great things.

I am worthy of all my biggest goals and dreams.

I am totally committed to making my goals a reality.

I can. I will. I must.

I can achieve anything I want.

I can do hard things.

I can do this, because I've got this.

I can accomplish anything I focus on.

Everything that I want is within my reach.

Everything I do turns into success.

I have what it takes to reach my goals.

I have what it takes to succeed and thrive.

I have what it takes to be successful in all that I do.

I have an abundance of opportunities to achieve my goals and dreams.

My success is now, and I am unstoppable.

Anything is possible for my life.

I am highly productive.

I am capable, consistent, and strong.

I am optimistic about my future.

I am focused and intentionally working towards my goals daily.

Achieving my goals allows me to live my best life.

I surpass all my goals with ease.

I am focused on completing all my action steps.

I step out of my comfort zone to achieve my goals.

I believe in myself and my abilities.

I release limits and boundaries.

I achieve more success than I can possibly imagine.

I take huge steps towards my goals each day.

I surround myself with people who encourage me to reach my goals.

I exercise discipline, patience, and perseverance.

I am daily growing into the person I need to be to achieve my goals.

Day after day I step closer to achieving my goals.

As long as I take action, I can achieve my goals.

What I am seeking is seeking me.

DAY 26

Affirmations for College Success

Education is the key to unlock the golden door of freedom.
-George Washington Carver

You don't have to have it all figured out to move forward.
-Joel Brown

I am a determined and talented student, and I will get accepted into college.

I am taking positive steps each day to reach my college goals.

I am thankful for the opportunity to attend college.

I am excited about the chance to be a college student.

I am reaching new levels by learning more each day.

I am improving my study habits each day.

I value my education because it prepares me for a bright future.

I study with a positive mindset and get good grades in all of my classes.

Professors and tutors are my resources. I won't hesitate to seek help if I need it.

Debt-free college is my goal. Early scholarship research is my strategy.

I am building a future filled with amazing opportunities and success.

I am becoming smarter every day and excelling in my exams.

I am looking forward to going to class every day and gaining knowledge.

I am discovering my passions and aligning them with my academic and career goals.

I am becoming more independent and self-reliant with each challenge I face.

I can balance my time between working a job in college and focusing on my studies.

I look forward to graduating college and adding value to society.

I will not give up on myself or academic goals, no matter the circumstances.

I am capable and determined to achieve my academic and personal goals.

I am assertive and confident, and I have everything I need to be successful.

I am actively embracing adulthood and learning to navigate the responsibilities.

I am thriving in my college journey, balancing academics, social life, and self-care.

I am thankful for my family, friends, and college support system.

I choose healthy ways to deal with stress.

I welcome college life and the great experiences it has to offer.

I have the discipline to stay focused while studying challenging subjects.

I have the discipline to take excellent notes in class that help me study later.

I begin studying well before exams are scheduled.

I strive to do my best every day and ace my exams.

I value my education because it opens doors to many opportunities.

I make a positive impact on other students' lives.

I am confident in my abilities to get excellent grades.

I am a responsible student accountable for all my choices and efforts.

My self-worth is not determined by my GPA. Failure is not final.

I believe in myself. I am capable of becoming a great student.

My mind's ability to learn and remember is increasing every day.

My education is the gateway to my future. Today I make the most of my academic opportunities.

My professors love having me as their student, and we get along great.

I press through stressful situations. My winner's mindset will help me succeed.

I am motivated to learn more, dig deeper, and conduct great research.

I am ready to become a stronger and better version of myself.

I am excited to go to college and get my degree.

I am grateful for my school, professors, and the opportunity to learn.

I am optimistic about finding a great roommate and a comfortable dorm environment.

Today, I choose not to worry about the future and focus on the present.

Today I set aside my fears and achieve all my educational goals.

I am committed to maintaining my faith, even if my college studies challenge some of my beliefs.

I trust in God's wisdom and strength to overcome academic obstacles.

I am grateful for God's provision and support throughout my college journey.

I am confident in God's plan for my future, including my college success.

DAY 27

Affirmations for Your Future Career

Pursue the things you love doing, and then do them so well that people can't take their eyes off you.
-Maya Angelou

Believe in yourself and all that you are. Know that there is something inside you that is greater than any obstacle.
-Christian D. Larson

I am going to be successful.

I am going to find a career that makes me happy.

I am capable of accomplishing anything I put my mind to.

I am surrounded by people who believe in me.

I am confident that I will find fulfillment and achieve success in my career.

I can succeed. I will succeed. I must succeed.

I can find a career that brings me joy and meaning.

Success begins with my mindset, and I choose to remain positive.

I have unique gifts and talents that will be a perfect match for my position.

I have confidence in my ability to make wise career decisions.

I have the humility to ask questions and receive the help I need in finding my career path.

I am confident that there is a bright future ahead of me.

I am surrounding myself with people who support my goals and dreams.

I am willing to put in the work needed to achieve my career goals.

I am ready for career success and eager to pursue valuable opportunities.

I will succeed in college and new opportunities will become abundant.

I will step out of my comfort zone.

I will transform failures into learning experiences.

I will be a valuable asset to my company/organization.

I will have the drive to pursue a promotion.

I will have a positive impact on people around me.

My talents will be valued and appreciated.

My presence will make a difference to my workplace.

My future job will give me awesome career opportunities, chances for promotion, and good pay.

I will achieve my career goals and find my dream job.

I will get attention from recruiters every day.

Every day I am better than before, and I leave all negativity behind.

Every day I deliver something of value and learn from my mistakes

I am willing to learn, grow, and continuously develop.

I am worthy of being paid highly for my time, skills, and effort.

I am proactive and get things done.

I am flexible and willing to change.

I am positive and optimistic.

I am the author of my own success story.

I am a natural born leader.

I release my limiting beliefs over my future career.

I release all doubts and embrace the belief that I can achieve.

I use challenges to create new opportunities.

I give myself permission to pursue the career I desire.

I embrace challenges as stepping stones to success.

I embrace change and rise to new opportunities.

I believe in myself and have confidence in my abilities.

There are lots of great opportunities that will be open to me.

Every interview will take me closer to my dream job.

I will set career goals and go after them with all the determination I can.

I will take advantage of every opportunity college has to offer.

I am consciously pushing myself to develop in all areas of my life.

I am surrounded and supported by smart, capable, and encouraging people.

I easily develop favor and rapport, creating genuine connections with everyone I meet.

I have everything I need to succeed, and if I don't, I will learn it.

Every day is a new opportunity to create my positive future.

I will have the skills I need to step up in my career.

I will align my career with my purpose and achieve great things.

I am open to amazing career opportunities.

College brings rewarding opportunities my way for my future career.

My potential is limitless, and I am going to make myself proud.

Thank you God for blessing and prospering my future career endeavors.

Affirmations to Level Up Your Productivity

DAY 28

Affirmations to Overcome Social Media and Gaming Dependence

Your time is valuable. Don't spend hours
scrolling through feeds that leave you feeling empty.
-Brené Brown

Beware of dream thieves such as social media, TV, video games,
negative people, procrastination, and overthinking.
-Lou Jones

I am not what I see online; I am much more than that. I am a unique individual.

I am an awesome person, inside and out and I don't compare myself to others.

I am choosing to prioritize activities that fuel my passions over video games.

I am in control of my online time, especially when it comes to gaming and social media.

I am in control of my social activities, and my excellent grades are proof of this.

I am ready to let go of old habits that no longer serve me.

I am taking action steps every day to be what I was created to be.

I am taking care of myself by getting enough sleep, eating well, and being physically active.

I am confident in my ability to keep my educational priorities number one.

I will never give out my personal information or location online, no matter what.

I will set limits for my online time to ensure it doesn't impact my sleep, studies, or social life.

I will use gaming as a way to relax and unwind after completing my tasks.

I will seek the support of my parents and counselors, if being online becomes a distraction.

I enjoy the benefits of gaming, like stress relief and social connection, while maintaining my priorities.

I will create a healthy balance between gaming and other important aspects of my life.

I forgive myself if I have allowed gaming and social media to negatively influence my grades.

I am capable of achieving better grades and will make the adjustments to do so.

I am not ashamed to seek the advice of parents and counselors to improve my situation.

I have the power to make all the necessary changes I need in my life.

I will always treat myself with the love, care, and the appreciation I deserve.

I free myself from what doesn't serve or value me.

I prioritize healthy relationships. When negativity arises, I walk away and seek environments that empower me.

Cyberbullying and harassment have no place in my life.

Video games don't control me. I take charge of my life.

My online world reflects my real-world values and morals, and I strive to live them in both worlds.

Each day is a gift, and I'm committed to making the most of it with passion and purpose.

It's important that I stay connected to people in the real world and not just digitally.

It's okay to game and be on social media, but it's not okay for it to control and hinder my life.

If someone online ever makes me feel uncomfortable, I will tell my parents immediately.

I use my computer in a practical and ethical way.

I improve my relationships with people who are important to me.

I am in control of my mind and will become the best version of me.

I am changing into someone who can control their impulses.

I focus my time on activities and relationships that empower my future.

I have the power to shake off any discouraging messages I receive on social media and in gaming chat rooms.

I love myself unconditionally, regardless of what I hear or see online.

I accept who I am, and I will not be defined by the opinions of others.

I feel good about myself and I refuse to compare myself to others online.

Gaming and social media can be fun, but I'll ensure they don't clash with my responsibilities.

My time is precious, and I choose to use it wisely.

I engage in the real world by discovering my purpose, volunteering in my community, and learning new skills.

I finish my homework before online activities and limit the time I spend online.

I overcome any obstacles that stand in the way of achieving a great life.

I work on developing my creativity and making education my top priority.

I have the strength to break free from social media or gaming dependence.

I celebrate every victory, big or small, in overcoming online distractions.

I take back my power; I'll make awesome choices moving forward.

DAY 29

Affirmations to Take Personal Responsibility

When you blame others, you give your power away.
When you take responsibility, you take
your power back to transform your life.
-Unknown

If it's never our fault, we can't take responsibility for it.
If we can't take responsibility for it, we'll always be its victim.
-Richard Bach

I am responsible.

I am responsible for my attitude.

I am responsible for my feelings.

I am responsible for my own happiness.

I am responsible for my health.

I am responsible for my belief in myself.

I am responsible for my financial health.

I am responsible for my success.

I am responsible for everything in my life.

I respond with ability.

I take responsibility for my past.

I take responsibility for my present.

I take responsibility for my future.

I take responsibility now.

Taking responsibility for my life empowers me.

Being responsible is one of my core values.

Today, I take 100% responsibility for my life.

I wake up, clean up, and show up.

I stand up, shape up, and grow up.

I am turning into someone who is competent, responsible, and self-reliant.

I celebrate my victories and embrace my failures as opportunities to learn and grow.

I am willing to do whatever it takes.

I am responsible for learning and gaining the skills, tools, and resources to live a better life.

I take responsibility for who I am–the good and bad.

I take responsibility for my choices and decisions.

I take responsibility for my set-backs and come-backs.

I step fully into personal responsibility.

I stand on my own two feet.

I am stable and trustworthy.

I keep my word.

I manage my money effectively and responsibly.

I earn my own money.

I am confident and secure.

I take control of my own life.

I show compassion to others.

I find it easy to do things for myself.

I accept responsibility for nurturing the gifts and strengths within me.

I accept responsibility for all of my choices.

I accept responsibility for my actions.

I choose to be accountable.

I support myself.

I use my time wisely and well.

I alone am responsible for how I act and react in any situation.

I am responsible for who I surround myself with.

I am responsible for what I allow from others.

I am responsible for what I accomplish in life.

I am responsible for the words that I speak.

I am responsible for my spending habits.

I am responsible for my daily habits.

I am responsible for my self-improvement.

I am responsible for nurturing my passions.

I am responsible for growing my spiritual walk.

I am responsible for growing in knowledge and increasing my understanding.

I am responsible for what I consume.

I am responsible for finding solutions to my problems.

I am responsible for all my thoughts, words, choices, and actions.

I take full responsibility for my life so that I may live my dreams.

DAY 30

Affirmations to Overcome Procrastination

Sometimes the smallest step in the right direction ends up being the biggest step of your life. Tiptoe if you must, but take a step.
-Naeem Callaway

Procrastination is the enemy of success.
-Unknown

I am a doer.

I am proactive.

I am disciplined.

I am grounded, focused, and attentive.

I am competent, committed, and diligent.

I am positive, proactive, and productive.

I am motivated to finish my tasks.

I do what needs doing even if it is hard or boring.

Fear cannot stop me.

Nothing will stand in my way of accomplishing my tasks and making progress.

I accept no excuses, just results.

The best time to start something new is right now.

All of my problems have solutions.

Although I make mistakes, I never quit.

Today, I abandon my old habits and take up new, more positive ones.

Today, I will take positive action towards my goals.

Today, I stop letting things distract me from reaching my goals.

Today, no matter what, I will focus on my number one priority.

Every small step I take makes a big difference.

Every day I am moving my life forward.

Every act of discipline creates more freedom for my future.

Everything I do today leads me to a better tomorrow.

I believe in myself and my abilities.

I believe my hard work is paying off.

By finishing my tasks now, I give my future self the gift of freedom.

By taking care of this present moment, I set myself up for a beautiful future.

I can do hard things.

I can do anything I set my mind to.

I can focus and concentrate at will.

I can accomplish everything that needs to get completed today.

I may make mistakes, but I don't quit.

I concentrate all my efforts on the things I want to accomplish in life.

I've got this.

I may stumble, but I never stay down.

I give myself permission to be imperfect.

I release negativity; Instead, I focus on positivity, productivity, and progress.

I release negative thoughts and choose to approach each task with confidence and positivity.

I choose to just get started rather than wait on perfect conditions.

I maximize the time I have.

I execute on the plans I've created.

I get things done fast.

I never put things off.

I tackle hard things first.

I work hard even though I may feel tired.

I work hard even when I don't feel like working.

My work ethic is stronger than my feelings.

My ability to conquer my challenges is limitless.

My potential to succeed is infinite.

My future self will thank me for all that I'm doing right now.

I love taking action.

I love taking action to accomplish my goals.

I am in control of my thoughts, choices, and actions.

I am committed to being focused on my goals because I am worth it.

I am equipped with all the tools I need to complete the task in front of me.

I am determined to get everything done.

I am not afraid to try and fail. I welcome the growth that comes from these experiences.

I am able to release negative thoughts and feelings that do not serve me.

I have the ability to focus on what needs to get done.

I have the willpower to complete my assignments.

I have clarity and energy.

I make time to do what's on my to do list.

I allow myself to focus on one small step at a time.

I will complete my number one priority today.

I will make good use of my time.

I take care of the future by taking care of the present.

I take one step at a time and get closer to completing my tasks.

I approach my tasks with confidence and enthusiasm.

I free myself from the paralysis of perfection.

I act quickly.

I hate wasting my time. I take immediate action.

I break all my goals into small, manageable steps.

I'm stronger than my procrastination.

I'm not afraid of doing hard things.

I'm excited to get this done and celebrate the results.

I'm getting closer to my dream life one day at a time.

DAY 31

Affirmations to Get a Job and Shine

A new job is an amazing chance to show the world
what you are capable of. You have everything to be great.
Just use it and never give up on your dreams.
-Unknown

Nothing worthwhile comes easily. Work, continuous work
and hard work, is the only way to accomplish results that last.
-Hamilton Holt

I am worthy of a new job.

I am the best person for this job.

I give myself permission to go after what I want.

I will find a job that I will enjoy having.

Everything always works out in my favor.

Every interview takes me closer to my ideal job.

Every rejection moves me closer to my ideal job.

I am worthy of every opportunity that comes my way.

I am talented enough to receive a job that I love.

I am patient, and I know that I will find the right job for me.

I am successful in everything I do.

I am positive, confident, and happy.

I am ready for a new fulfilling job now.

My resume stands out and easily gets me an interview.

I am going to rock my next job interview.

I am ready for a constant stream of income.

Lots of new job opportunities are coming my way.

It's easy for me to find a new job that I love.

I only receive rewarding next-level offers that exceed my highest expectations.

The job search process is fun and easy for me.

I find it easy to network with others and make meaningful connections.

I walk in a spirit of excellence.

I am committed to finding a new job that will be fulfilling and interesting.

I am confident that I have the right skill set to land the right job with great pay.

This job will not define my worth or who I am.

I am open to an amazing position that will fulfill my money expectations.

I am worthy of receiving a job that I love.

I am open and receptive to all job opportunities.

I have what it takes to do well on my job interview.

I can transform obstacles into opportunities.

I am not afraid to put myself out there.

Employers are eagerly looking for me.

My skills are in high demand.

I'm one step closer to my ideal job with every action I take.

I deserve to be paid well for my skills.

I will land a job with a great supervisor and team.

I trust God with all my heart for wonderful, new job opportunities.

Bonus Chapters

Affirmations for Abundance and Prosperity

There are many roads to prosperity, but one must be taken.
Inaction leads nowhere.
-Robert Zoellick

If you want to be financially free, you need
to become a different person than you are today
and let go of whatever has held you back in the past.
-Robert Kiyosaki

I am the creator of generational wealth.

I am a generational curse breaker.

I am worthy of a future full of prosperity.

Abundance is my birthright.

All of my actions lead to abundance and prosperity.

All my thoughts lead to diligence and plenty.

All resistance to money is gone from my life.

All the time I dedicate to my dreams is going to pay off.

I am worthy of the wealth I desire.

I am capable of achieving success.

I can overcome any financial obstacles.

I am an excellent money manager.

I am blessed and highly favored.

I am generous with my money.

I am a great giver and an excellent receiver.

I am a channel for money to flow to and through.

I am at peace with having a lot of money.

I am prosperous and successful in all that I do.

I have knowledge and understanding of money and making money.

I am financially free and debt free.

I am capable of success and wealth.

I have whatever I need to succeed.

I have more than enough to meet all my needs and desires and to be a blessing.

I have all that I need, and I generously share my success with others.

I have peace beyond understanding, and I walk in all abundance designed for me.

I have an abundant mindset.

I release negative thoughts about money.

I am prosperous, and I will continue to be prosperous.

I leave an inheritance for generations to come.

I am thankful for abundance and prosperity coming to pass in my life.

I am confident in all that I am, all that I have, and all that I can do.

I am willing and able to create wealth.

I am making financial progress.

AFFIRMATIONS FOR ABUNDANCE AND PROSPERITY

I am worthy of wealth and able to enjoy it.

My dreams will come true.

My income is always increasing.

My giving is always increasing.

My actions create constant wealth.

My life is full of wealth opportunities.

My current circumstances do not affect my desired reality. I stay focused on the life I want.

My life will not revolve around money, because I am secure.

I possess money, but money does not possess me.

I look for wise investment opportunities and ways to bless others financially.

I give generously and even more is given back to me.

My financial freedom is within reach.

I make money doing what I love.

I am patient in building wealth and never resort to get-rich-quick schemes.

I achieve my financial goals.

I accept and receive unexpected money.

I spend money wisely and with a purpose.

I live from a place of abundance.

I boldly conquer my money goals.

I see wealth opportunities everywhere.

I release all resistance to wealth.

I create prosperity easily and effortlessly.

I always have enough money.

I give myself permission to be wealthy and successful.

I receive prosperous ideas and act on them with ease.

I openly share the wealth I receive.

I embrace new avenues of income.

I am a wise steward with money.

I am skilled at making passive income and maximize multiple channels for increase.

I educate myself to know how to handle money well.

I deserve to make more money.

I see myself living in limitless abundance.

Money comes to me in abundance in expected and unexpected ways.

Money creates a positive impact on my life.

There is a clear path before me to abundance.

Favorable circumstances await me. I am excited to receive them.

Yes, my finances are secure, and they will continue to grow with ease.

Everything I want is on its way to me in due time.

Opportunities are coming and will continue to come to me.

Everything I need to succeed is already within me.

All things work out for my good.

It's never too late to turn my dreams into reality.

I focus on ways to make a lot of money easily.

I honor God with all my income.

I am a willing vessel God uses to spread love, kindness, and abundant generosity.

I open my heart to accept all the abundance God has for me.

I wake up peacefully, knowing that God is taking care of me.

God has blessed me with the ability to attain wealth through my skill set.

Affirmations for Entrepreneurial Success

The best way to predict the future is to create it.
-Peter Drucker

What do you need to start a business? Three simple things: know your product better than anyone, know your customer, and have a burning desire to succeed.
-Dave Thomas

I am an entrepreneur.

I am successful.

I am confident in my brand and mission.

I am confident in my ability to create wealth.

I am highly successful and passionate at what I do.

I am great at solving people's pain points and offering them solutions of great value.

I am serving my life's purpose through my business.

I am increasingly confident in my ability to create the life I desire.

My ideas generate wealth and prosperity.

My brand is clear, authentic, and powerful.

My expertise and hard work earn me great profits.

My work makes a positive difference.

My potential is limitless.

I learn as I go.

I can and I will do this. Nothing can stop me.

I turn my expertise into income.

I focus my energy on what I'm good at.

The more I give, the more I receive.

The right mentors help me excel in reaching my entrepreneurship goals.

There are no limits to what I can achieve.

This does not need to be perfect.

This is going to be a great day.

I am worthy of my dreams and goals.

I am creating a life I deserve to live.

I am committed to doubling my income and beyond.

I am 100% committed to my success.

I am a powerful creator.

I am in charge of my efforts and success.

I am capable and confident in running a successful, prosperous business.

I am inspired and motivated.

I am always striving for progress, not perfection.

I got this.

I offer the best product/service that money can buy.

I believe in myself and my abilities.

I believe I can achieve greatness.

I give up my limiting beliefs on money.
I give myself permission to become wealthy.
Entrepreneurship is a path of prosperity for me.
I am paid richly for my skills, services, and products.
All I need to do is take the next tiny step.
Self-doubt has no place in my life.
I reject all imposter syndrome.
Now is my time.
My goals are possible.
My business is flourishing.
My knowledge is profitable.
My income is constantly increasing.
My sacrifices are leading to prosperity and wealth.
I make a difference.
I make a positive impact in what I do.
I make tough decisions and do hard things when I have to.
I do not worry about the things I cannot control.
I release my doubts and insecurities.
I use my competition as inspiration.
I allow creativity to flow through me with ease.
I lead with integrity, passion, and care.
I see every setback as a chance to make a comeback.
I place no limits on the amount of money I can make.
I provide products and services that people need.
I have the ability to create absolutely anything I want.

I invest in myself and my business every day.

I deserve to be financially free.

I love what I do.

I believe that I can make a difference.

I create a wonderful life for me and my family.

I overcome hurdles and difficulties with ease.

I will not settle for less.

The more I learn, the more successful I can be.

Today, I am going to be better than yesterday.

When one door closes, another one opens for me.

Money flows into my business easily and effortlessly.

What I focus on grows, and so I focus on my business.

I am creating generational wealth.

I am persistent in all that I do.

I am getting closer to fulfilling my dreams.

I am building a powerful and positive business.

I am capable of creating success.

I am great at time management and people leadership.

I am learning and growing as an entrepreneur.

I am driven by passion and purpose.

I am worthy of financial security.

I receive my ideal customers/clients.

My clients/customers love my business and become raving fans.

I am worthy of success.

All my goals are coming to pass.

It's okay to take breaks and rest my body and mind.

It's okay to make mistakes, and I will not let them hinder me.

My dreams are becoming reality.

My actions create constant prosperity.

My business changes lives.

My business is a massive success.

I make money while I sleep.

I speak confidently about my business.

I create the life I want.

If it's to be, it begins with me.

I trust God to reward my efforts with success.

I step back and let God lead the way.

Affirmations for Staying Focused

I don't care how much power, brilliance or energy you have,
if you don't harness it and focus it on a specific target,
and hold it there you're never going to accomplish
as much as your ability warrants.
-Zig Ziglar

Where focus goes, energy flows.
And if you don't take the time to focus on what matters,
then you're living a life of someone else's design.
-Tony Robbins

I am focused on the task at hand.

I am present.

I am not distracted.

I am an expert at time management.

I am alert and attentive at all times.

I am free of confusion.

My mind is clear and focused.

My concentration grows stronger every day.

My attention is undivided.

By focusing on the best things in my life, I give them power to grow and multiply.

Focusing on the present moment improves my concentration and productivity.

Giving each moment my undivided attention, creates endless inspiration for me.

Because I am focused on what I am doing, I get the results I desire.

I easily concentrate on every task I perform.

I easily get into the flow whenever required.

I release scattered thoughts and return my focus to the present moment.

I ignore everything that attempts to disturb my concentration and momentum.

I focus my mind easily and quickly.

I focus my attention on my top priorities in life.

I focus my mind only on those things which are aligned with my goals.

I focus my thoughts on what I want, and I take action towards that purpose.

I focus my priorities on success and prosperity.

My concentrated efforts are paying off.

My focus is a key to my success.

Right now, I focus only on this priority.

Nothing distracts me.

Being focused comes easily to me.

As long as I keep my thoughts on my goals, I easily maintain my focus and momentum.

Because my life is clutter-free, my mind is clear, attentive, and focused.

Being in the zone is something I strive to attain and maintain every day.

I am fully focused and present in all interactions with others.

I am focused on realizing all of my dreams.

I keep my thoughts on my goals.

I free myself from distractions.

I have a singular focus.

I give myself permission to turn off whatever is distracting me.

I have clarity and energy.

I center my thoughts on what I am doing.

I will accomplish everything I need to do today.

I commit myself to developing the highest level of focus in my life.

I do one task at a time.

I seek improvement, not perfection.

I can focus my attention at will.

I can do what needs to be done.

I focus on each activity throughout my day.

I focus on the end result.

I focus on excellence in all that I do.

I am focused and in my zone.

Affirmations for Letting Go of Stress, Worry, and Anxiety

It's not the load that breaks you down, it's the way you carry it.
-Lou Holtz

Stress is caused by your thoughts, not the situation.
-Unknown

I am not my anxiety.

I am free from stress.

I am able to let go of anxiety and worry.

I am letting go of all my worries and fears.

I am able to release negativity and let go of stress.

I let go of all negative emotions.

I am in control of my mind and will become focused and worry-free.

I release any tension in my body from stress.

I release worst-case scenario thinking.

I don't need to worry about things I can't control.

I have the strength to move beyond my anxiety.

I have the power to overcome my doubts, worries, and fears.

I have the power to make all the necessary changes I need in my life.

Challenges are opportunities for me to grow.

This situation will pass. Everything is temporary.

Today, I'll do the best that I can.

I don't judge myself.

I release the past.

I free myself from what doesn't serve me or value me.

I will not only survive, I will thrive.

I overcome any obstacles in my way.

I will not be held back by worry and negative thoughts.

This stressful experience does not define who I am.

This feeling and situation is temporary.

I am far stronger than I realize.

I am able to overcome anything in my life.

I am safe and supported.

I am right where I need to be.

I am calm and full of joy.

I am releasing all negative emotions from my life.

I am a positive person who brings positive things into my life.

I know my worth is high.

I deserve a peaceful and loving life.

I have nothing to be anxious about.

I free myself from fear of the unknown.

I will not worry about money.

AFFIRMATIONS FOR LETTING GO OF STRESS, WORRY, AND ANXIETY

I take things one step at a time.

Today, and every day, I choose joy.

Releasing stress is easy.

I give myself space to be free.

I choose to think positive, nurturing thoughts.

I know that constant worrying is not helping to improve the outcome.

I focus my energy on my values, not my anxiety.

I have the ability to re-evaluate and overcome this stressful situation.

I accept and love myself unconditionally.

Affirmations for Better Self-Care

Self-care is a priority and necessity, not a luxury.
-Unknown

Almost everything will work again if you unplug it
for a few minutes, including you.
-Anne Lamott

I am worth taking care of.

I am well-rested and full of energy.

I am powerful, healthy, and capable.

I am one-of-a-kind, and there is no one else like me.

I am worthy of love from myself and others.

I am investing in my future self.

I am overflowing with love, joy, happiness, and peace.

I make sure I get enough water.

I make sure I get enough exercise.

I deserve to treat myself well.

I deserve the best care.

I deserve the best and will not settle for anything less.

Taking care of myself is my first responsibility.

Taking care of myself brings me happiness.

Taking care of myself is loving.

Taking care of myself makes me smart.

I give myself permission to fail.

I give myself permission to succeed.

I give myself permission to release toxic thoughts.

I give myself permission to rest.

I enjoy my body and take good care of it.

I speak positively to myself.

I praise and encourage myself.

I stop myself from self-blame.

I am happy to be me.

I am relaxed and at peace.

I am what I need.

I am safe.

I am my biggest cheerleader.

I am worry-free.

I am getting better and better.

I am strong, unique, and smart.

I respect myself.

I care for myself daily.

I live my life without self-imposed limitations.

I release myself of any misery and suffering.

I release thoughts that drain me and refocus my energy on thoughts that empower me.

I will turn negative thoughts into positive ones.

I will not let negativity tear me down.

I will practice self-mercy and kindness.

I give myself grace.

I will take action and accomplish my goals.

I will try new things.

I will be kind to myself today.

I give myself proper nutrition.

I give myself time.

My worth doesn't depend on how I look.

I take excellent care of myself.

I take care of my body, soul, and spirit.

I like myself, so I care for myself.

I always make sure to take care of myself first.

I will do my best for myself.

I accept myself for who I am.

Today, I will be better to myself than yesterday.

Today, I choose self-love instead of self-hatred.

I love myself, and I like myself too.

I love myself and the life I'm building.

I love myself for who I am, and my flaws are part of my perfection.

I push myself a little harder each day to reach my health goals.

I cheer myself on.

I have the power to make the right choices for me.

Toxic things and people have no place in my life.

It's okay for me to have fun.

It's okay for me to pamper myself.

It's okay for me to splurge on myself once in a while.

It's okay to feel good.

It's okay if things don't go as planned.

Healthy food fuels my body.

If I fail, I will fail forward.

The only person who can change me is me.

When I let go, I create space for something new or something better.

My life is a gift and I treat it accordingly.

My self-care is my priority, no matter how busy I am.

Affirmations for Healing a Broken Heart

To be rejected by someone doesn't mean you should also reject yourself or that you should think of yourself as a lesser person.
-Jocelyn Soriano

Every time I thought I was being rejected from something good, I was actually being re-directed to something better.
-Steve Maraboli

I am valuable and worthy.

I am able to heal.

I am lovable.

I am okay.

I am letting go of what doesn't serve me.

I am open to the possibility that this relationship was not in my best interest.

I am on my way to something even better.

I am free to be the best version of me

I am free to begin again.

I release my past.

I release these chains.

I release myself from all regrets and disappointments.

I matter, no matter how I feel.

I know my worth, even if someone else doesn't.

I choose to have the strength to move on.

I choose to let go of this anger.

I choose happiness today instead of dwelling on my past disappointments.

I love and accept myself no matter what.

I love myself unconditionally.

This pain is temporary.

This pain will lessen.

I will get through this.

I will heal from this.

I will love again when the time is right.

I will find joy in life again.

I will love myself the way I deserve to be loved.

I will take time away for personal and spiritual growth.

There is no relationship loss that I cannot overcome.

I do not deserve abuse.

Healing begins within me.

I forgive myself.

I forgive myself unconditionally.

I forgive myself for all the mistakes I've made.

I forgive the person that hurt me.

My heart will heal, and I will have peace.

My breakup is an opportunity for me to be free and live my best life.

It's time to let go of them and let go of bitterness.

I stand firm on my principles and values.

I have a lot to offer, and I am enough.

I have faith that there is a divine plan for my love life.

I am open to only healthy and positive relationships.

I am blessed because I am moving on.

I am excited about this new beginning.

I am worthy of love and respect.

I am more than this breakup.

I am strong enough to heal from this broken heart.

I trust that this ending is for my highest good.

It's perfectly normal to feel this way after a breakup.

I am grateful for the lessons.

I am completely whole and perfect by myself.

I am deserving of love.

I am complete on my own.

I am healing more and more every day.

I am working on me, for me.

My life is full of blessings. I look forward to tomorrow.

I trust that everything will work out for my good.

It is getting easier day by day.

There is someone amazing waiting for me.

No matter what happens in my life, I still love myself.

I find strength in God and know God has a plan for my love life.

The best is yet to come.

Affirmations for Letting Go and Moving Forward

Pain will leave you, when you let go.
-Jeremy Aldana

Accept yourself, love yourself, and keep moving forward.
If you want to fly, you have to give up what weighs you down.
-Roy T. Bennett

I am free.

I am free from worry.

I am free of the pain.

I am free of burdens.

I am free from my past mistakes.

I am free to be me.

I let go.

I let go of pain.

I let go of anger.

I let go of regrets.

I let go of fear.

I let go of past relationships that are not right for me.

I release the grudges I held in the past, and I am free.

I release all the baggage that has stopped me from moving forward.

I release the burden of shame, guilt, and self-judgment.

I release all stress and criticisms.

I forgive myself and let go of all the feelings and mindsets that hold me back.

I forgive those who have harmed me in the past and peacefully detach from them.

I forgive those who wronged me.

I choose not to be around people who make me feel worthless or unhappy.

I don't need toxic people in my life.

I love and accept my family members exactly as they are.

I unconditionally love my family even if they do not understand me completely.

I am healing at my own pace, and I will be at peace.

I am healed and whole.

I am not afraid to move on.

I am accepting of my imperfections.

I am capable of loving all of who I am.

I am not my past.

I am letting go of the past.

I am over it.

I am so much more than my past mistakes.

I am empowered to live free when I let go.

I am ready to let go and move on with my life.

I am leaving the past behind and pressing forward.

I am letting go of everything that stresses me out.

I am focusing on the positive and shifting towards a happier mindset.

I let go of resentment and any other feeling that doesn't positively help me.

I let go of the need to control others.

I let go of all unrealistic expectations.

I let go of all urges to criticize myself.

I can face challenges and stand back up after a setback.

I can overcome everything that comes my way.

My spirit is renewed and free.

My past does not define me.

My mind is free from distractions.

My strength is greater than any struggle.

I embrace this new season of my life.

I live my life without restraints.

I allow myself to be forgiven.

I choose to take time for myself.

I have struggled enough, and it ends today.

I will stop worrying and find a solution.

I stop holding things against others.

I say goodbye to all the negativity.

I say goodbye to things that block my mental and spiritual growth.

I will not let the pain of the past keep me from moving forward.

I free myself from fear of the unknown.

I overcome self-condemnation and choose to love myself unconditionally.

I let go of everything that worries me.

I choose freedom and release all things that block my blessings.

I have learned all the lessons, and I'm ready to let go.

I have the power to let go of my past and move on.

I move beyond my mistakes.

I focus solely on what I can control and let go of what I cannot.

I leave behind the old me and embrace the new me.

I'm open to a better future.

I choose to thrive and enjoy my life.

I hold on to the positive memories and let go of negative ones.

Letting go of my pain helps me heal.

I am not my past. I let go and let God.

I am worthy of God's best for my life.

ABOUT THE AUTHOR ✧

Lou Jones is a speaker, life coach, minister of the gospel, and former youth pastor who motivates audiences of all ages. Through powerful keynotes, workshops, and coaching sessions he has helped thousands transform their lives. Drawing on his own personal trials and triumphs, Lou inspires and equips people to live their lives to the fullest and maximize their potential. He lives in Dallas, Texas, with his wife, Ruth, and their son Aiden.

- @loujonesinspires
- @loujonesinspires
- @loujonesinspires
- @loujonesinspires
- @loujonesinspires
- @loujonesinspire
- loujones.com

ACKNOWLEDGEMENTS

I'm deeply grateful to you, God, for the inspiration to write this book. For over a year, I sought your guidance, fervently listening for your direction and the specific book I was meant to write. When I was sensitive enough to hear you, your response surprised me—not just one book, but multiple. I am eternally at your service, and my heart overflows with gratitude.

To begin this journey of gratitude, I want to acknowledge the incredible strength embodied in a woman I hold dear—my mother, Gloria Jones. You've transcended the role of a parent; you've been my friend, mentor, wise counselor, supporter, and encourager. The unstoppable man I am today owes its existence to you.

To my remarkable wife, Ruth, you stand as a testament to God's faithfulness in my life. What I believed for, you've exceeded beyond my wildest expectations. You are my inspiration, confidant, biggest cheerleader, partner, and strategist. As the first author in our family, you've paved the way, contributing as my editor, designer, and publisher. Because of your sacrifice, this book has been published, as testimony to the collaborative strength that defines our life together. You are the greatest wife and friend a man could ask for. Thank you for being such a wonderful mother to our son, Aiden, and for being the glue that holds our beautiful family together.

Aiden, my lion-like leader—my son—you bring immeasurable blessing to my life. I can't imagine life without you, and I'm honored to be your father. Thank you for your unconditional love.

A heartfelt shout-out to my Detroit circle of friends—Ajay, Carl and April, Vern and Erica, Sheronda, Kim, Deidre, Monique, and many others. I remember when you all blessed me with a silver bracelet engraved with "Pastor Lou" on the front and "Entrusted to Lead" on the back. Your support and encouragement still resonate in my spirit.

To my Phoenix friends, especially my Phoenix mother June, thank you for your love and support. Quintin, your friendship and support has been a true blessing in my life. Thank you for helping me step into my entrepreneurial gift.

The roots of my connection to affirmations trace back to my beloved high school history teacher, Mr. Robert Lichtman. Thank you for introducing me to the unstoppable influence of affirmations, fostering not only my leadership skills but also my passion for education.

To the numerous friends and family who've shaped my life's path, your kind words, belief in me, and unwavering support are etched in my heart and prayers.

Finally, to everyone who has been part of my journey, whether online followers or those I've met in person, my God-given mission is you. I aim to inspire and equip you to reach your fullest potential. May this book be a catalyst, helping you level up in life and become unstoppable.

REFERENCES

Cooke, R., Trebaczyk, H., Harris, P., & Wright, A.J. (2014) Self-affirmation promotes physical activity. Journal of Sport and Exercise Psychology, 36(2), 217–223.

Critcher, C. R., & Dunning, D. (2015). Self-affirmations provide a broader perspective on self-threat. Personality and Social Psychology Bulletin, 41(1), 3-18.

Epton, T., & Harris, P.R. (2008). Self-affirmation promotes health behavior change. Health Psychology, 27(6), 746-752.

Gu, R., Yang, J., Yang, Z. et al. Self-affirmation enhances the processing of uncertainty: An event-related potential study. Cogn Affect Behav Neurosci 19, 327–337 (2019). https://doi.org/10.3758/s13415-018-00673-0

Harris, P. R., Mayle, K., Mabbott, L., & Napper, L. (2007). Self-affirmation reduces smokers' defensiveness to graphic on-pack cigarette warning labels. Health Psychology, 26, 437–446.

Koole, S.L., Smeets, K., van Knippenberg, A., Dijksterhuis, A. (1999). The cessation of rumination through self-affirmation. Journal of Personality and Social Psychology, 77, 111–125.

Layous, K., Davis, E. M., Garcia, J., Purdie-Vaughns, V., Cook, J. E., & Cohen, G. L. (2017). Feeling left out, but affirmed: Protecting against the negative effects of low belonging in college. Journal of Experimental Social Psychology, 69, 227-231.

Logel, C., & Cohen, G.L. (2012). The role of the self in physical health: Testing the effect of a values-affirmation intervention on weight loss. Psychological Science, 23(1), 53–55.

Sherman, D. K., Cohen, G. L., Nelson, L. D., Nussbaum, A. D., Bunyan, D. P., & Garcia, J. (2009). Affirmed yet unaware: Exploring the role of awareness in the process of self-affirmation. Journal of Personality and Social Psychology, 97, 745-764.

Wiesenfeld, B.M., Brockner, J., Petzall, B., Wolf, R., & Bailey J. (2001). Stress and coping among layoff survivors: A self-affirmation analysis. Anxiety, Stress and Coping: An International Journal, 14, 15–34.

YOUR LIFE, MINDSET, AND SPIRIT

with the Unstoppable Motivation on Demand Bundle

Get your bundle now:

loujones.com/unstoppable

Boost your awesome with our super cool tools!
Get ready to feel fired up, conquer challenges like a champ, and rock your world with confidence!

EMPOWER YOUR DAY WITH AFFIRMATIONS!

OVER 30 TOPICS INCLUDING:

FOR AGES 18+

- STRESS & ANXIETY
- SELF-LOVE
- CONFIDENCE
- WEIGHT-LOSS
- BODY IMAGE
- HEALTH & HEALING
- SUCCESS AT WORK
- ABUNDANCE
- LANDING A NEW JOB
- BROKEN HEART
- LOVE & RELATIONSHIPS

www.ingramcontent.com/pod-product-compliance
Lightning Source LLC
Chambersburg PA
CBHW072153070526
44585CB00015B/1126